T0065773

She's beautiful,

she's talented,

she's famous.

She's a star!

Things would be perfect if only her family was around to help her celebrate. . . .

Follow **Star's** adventures in

a new series from **Aladdin Paperbacks!**

#1 Supernova

#2 Always Dreamin'

#3 Never Give Up

#4 Together We Can Do It

#5 Blast from the Past

#6 Someday, Some Way

#7 Over the Top

Look for the next book in the series

#8 Star Bright

star power

#7

Over the Top

Catch Star's act!

 #1 Supernova

 **#2 Always Dreamin'**

 **#3 Never Give Up**

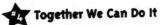 **#4 Together We Can Do It**

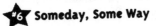 **#5 Blast from the Past**

 **#6 Someday, Some Way**

#7 Over the Top

A new book drops every other month!
Next up:

#8 Star Bright

From Aladdin Paperbacks
Published by Simon & Schuster

#7

star power

Over the Top

by Catherine Hapka

Aladdin Paperbacks
New York London Toronto Sydney

This book is a work of fiction. Any references to historical events, real people, or real locales are used fictitiously. Other names, characters, places, and incidents are the product of the author's imagination, and any resemblance to actual events or locales or persons, living or dead, is entirely coincidental.

ALADDIN PAPERBACKS
An imprint of Simon & Schuster Children's Publishing Division
1230 Avenue of the Americas, New York, NY 10020
Copyright © 2005 by Catherine Hapka
All rights reserved, including the right of
reproduction in whole or in part in any form.
ALADDIN PAPERBACKS and colophon are registered trademarks of
Simon and Schuster, Inc.
Designed by Tom Daly
The text of this book was set in Triplex.
Manufactured in the United States of America
First Aladdin Paperbacks edition March 2005
2 4 6 8 10 9 7 5 3 1
Library of Congress Control Number 2004107436
ISBN 978-0-689-87669-1   ISBN 0-689-87669-6

One

"Are you finished with my eye shadow yet, Lola?" Star Calloway asked. "I don't see why I have to look so glam for this thing, anyway. I'm not the guest of honor—nobody's going to be looking at me."

Star's stylist, Lola LaRue, picked another shade of shimmering makeup out of the jumble of bottles and tubes strewn across the small tabletop in the tour-bus kitchenette. "Don't count on it, sugar," she replied with a chuckle, pushing back her own fuchsia-tinted dreadlocks before bending down and grasping Star gently by the chin to steady her face. "Half the music industry is going to be at this soiree. That means major paparazzi crawling around everywhere—you'll need to look your most adorable for the pictures."

Feeling a bit befuddled at the idea that in the music business even a funeral could turn into a glamorous event, Star stayed motionless as her stylist got back to work. The tour bus had long since emerged from the tunnel that ran beneath the English Channel. Star knew that she and her entourage would soon be arriving in London, where the funeral of Ernie "The Ear" Golden, a hugely successful music producer, would be taking place in a couple of days.

After almost two years as an international singing sensation, Star was starting to get used to the kind of lifestyle most fourteen-year-old girls could hardly imagine in their wildest dreams. But at certain moments it all still seemed a little unreal to her. For instance, every time she stepped onto her super-luxurious tour bus, with its sumptuous furnishings, its state-of-the-art entertainment system, and its framed gold records decorating the walls between tinted windows, Star felt a tiny shiver of surprise—*Is all this really mine?*

She had seen a lot of that tour bus lately. Star and her entourage had been crisscrossing their way from one end of Europe to the other over the past few months, with sold-out concerts at every stop.

Her manager, Mike Mosley, who was sitting across the table, stood up and stretched. At almost six and a half feet tall, he made even the spacious tour bus seem a little cramped.

"Lola's right, darlin'," he told Star, rubbing his mustache. "The whole world is going to be watchin' this funeral. Ernie Golden was more than just a producer; the ol' galoot was pretty much a star himself. That's how important he's been to the music biz."

Lola nodded so hard that her dangling doughnut-size rhinestone earrings jingled. "That's why they called him 'The Ear,'" she added. "He discovered or signed more talent than most people have in their CD collections."

"I know, I know," Star said with a smile. "You guys have been telling me that kind of stuff since we left Amsterdam. And I totally get it—I mean, I'd definitely heard of Mr. Golden even before I got signed and everything. He was, like, a legend." She shrugged. "That's why I figure nobody will really be looking at me. Everyone will want to pay attention to the funeral and stuff, right?"

Before either of the adults could answer, Star's tutor came down the aisle toward them, swaying slightly with the motion of the bus. Magdalene Nattle, better known as Mags, had been up front talking to Star's bodyguard, Tank Massimo, who was driving. "Tank says we should be arriving at the hotel in about twenty minutes," Mags reported, running a hand over her salt-and-pepper hair.

"Thanks, Mrs. Nattle," Star said. "We'll be ready. Maybe."

Lola smiled calmly. "Yes, we will," she agreed. "But only if a certain someone stops wriggling and lets me do my job."

Star grinned, doing her best to keep still. Glancing out the tinted window while Lola reached for an eyelash curler, she saw that the bus was trundling through the city streets. It felt strange to be back in London, where her world tour had kicked off all those weeks earlier. Sometimes Star felt as if she had been on the road for ages, while at other times it seemed as if the tour had just started yesterday. Either way Star knew that she had changed a lot since those first shows. After so many performances in so many different countries, the specifications of her concert—the song list, the dance moves, even some of the patter between songs—felt as familiar as it had once felt to stop at her locker before moving on to homeroom back at New Limpet Middle School.

Guess it's true what Dad always told me, Star thought. *We human beings are amazing—we can get used to just about anything.*

Her hand strayed to the silver star pendant she always wore on a slim chain around her neck. It had been a gift from her parents—one of the last gifts she'd received from them. Two years ago, just as Star's singing career was about to take off, her parents and baby brother had disappeared during a boat trip in Florida. The police still didn't know what had become of them, though Star had never given up hope that they would be found one day, safe and sound. In the meantime she was grateful to Mike, Mags, Tank, and the others on her team for taking over as her second family. She knew that her parents, when they returned, would be grateful too.

Star was jolted out of those thoughts as the bus bounced over a particularly deep pothole. "Yipes," she blurted out, jerking her head back before Lola's eyelash curler could poke her in the eye. Mike stumbled, catching himself on the back of the banquette, while Mags grabbed the edge of the table.

"Sorry about that, gang," Tank called from the driver's seat.

Mike grumbled, pushing himself upright. Then he sat down again across from Star and Lola, reaching for a thick newspaper that was lying on the bench beside him. He spread it out on the tabletop, resting his elbows on the edge as he glanced down at the front page. "Check it out, y'all," he said. "Here's another article about . . ."

His Texas-tinged voice trailed off as Star's dog, a chubby fawn pug named Dudley Do-Wrong, appeared out of nowhere and jumped onto Mike's lap, and then onto the table. Letting out a moist snort of contentedness, Dudley flopped down right on top of the newspaper.

"Scat, you mangy mutt," Mike growled at the dog, poking

Dudley in his round belly. "You make a better door than window, you know."

Star giggled. "Don't be a meanie, Mike," she said. "Dudsters wants to read about the Golden Ear, too."

Mike rolled his eyes as he gently shoved Dudley off the paper and onto the bench beside Star. "He'll have a hard time reading through that overfed behind of his."

"What's this article say?" Lola asked, briefly reaching over to scratch Dudley's head. The dog was resting his chin on the table, staring at Mike with his brown eyes bulging and his pink tongue lolling out of his mouth.

Mike scanned the page. "Mostly the same stuff as all the rest," he said. "Goes over Golden's career, talks about how he was the one who discovered Jefferson Black and Athena Quincy and all sorts of other icons back in the day, and then how he eventually started his own company. How he never lost his touch for a new sound, even as old as he was—he was the one who signed Tween Scene just last year, you know. Oh, and how his motto for life was *carpe diem*."

"Carp-hey-what?" Star wrinkled her nose. "You're starting to sound like Tank now," she joked, glancing toward the front of the bus, where one of her bodyguard's muscular arms was visible poking out from the driver's seat. Many people misjudged Tank as a mindless meathead, but in reality he was one of the smartest and most thoughtful people Star had ever met. He had traveled all over the world, and he spoke at least seventeen foreign languages.

"Oh, Star," Mags said with a 'tut-tut' expression on her face. "Have I taught you nothing? *'Carpe diem'* is a Latin phrase, first attributed to the ancient Roman poet Horace and meaning, roughly, 'seize the day.' It's generally used to express the idea that one should enjoy the present without letting worries about the future get in the way."

"That's right," Mike put in, still staring down at the newspaper photo of Golden. "And that's what Ernie tried to do every day of his life."

Star noticed that her manager's voice sounded subdued and sort of sad. Though she had only met Ernie Golden a few times herself, she knew that Mike had known and respected him for years. Golden had seemed like a man who loved music more than anything else, and that made Star feel a kinship with him. She was glad she would have a chance to pay her respects.

"I wonder if Athena Quincy will be at the funeral," she said, her fingers seeking out her star pendant again. Star's parents adored Athena Quincy's music. They had even named their daughter after one of the diva's well-known hits, "Star Bright." The song—and Athena—had always been special to Star. However, although Star had met countless celebrities since becoming one herself, she had yet to meet Athena in person.

Mike was still staring down at the newspaper. "Looks that way," he reported. "There's a list here of celebrities expected to attend."

"Who?" Lola asked curiously, glancing up from Star's lashes.

"Oh, the usual suspects," Mike said with a shrug. "Athena and Jefferson, Eddie Urbane, Charleston Rock, Jade, the kids from Boysterous and Tween Scene . . ."

"Wow," Star said. "Sounds like the list for the Notey Awards or something."

Mike smiled. "You're mentioned too, sweetheart," he told Star. "So prepare yourself. This whole shindig'll prob'ly be more like the Noteys than any funeral you've ever seen. Tonight's the welcome party, which is takin' place at our hotel—prob'ly be crawlin' with paparazzi. Then tomorrow night there's s'posed to be a big black-tie memorial show, with PopTV filming and whatnot. And finally the funeral itself is the following day."

"Wow, sounds like they'll be keeping us busy," Star commented. "Lucky this whole thing happened at the same time we were scheduled to be on break from the tour for a few days."

"Yeah," Lola grumbled as she dug through her makeup kit. "Lucky us. Instead of learning to snowboard and sipping hot cocoa in the Alps, we get to hang out at a three-day funeral."

Star smiled at her, knowing that Lola didn't really mind giving up her mini-vacation for such an important occasion. Besides, they'd all had a two-week break a short while earlier, right before the whirlwind schedule of shows they'd just finished in Denmark, Belgium, and the Netherlands.

Mike rubbed his bushy mustache thoughtfully. "We won't just be missing out on the R&R," he said. "We're also going to have to make up those extra rehearsals and musician meetings and whatnot that we were plannin' to fit in this week."

Star nodded. Even though her tour was scheduled to go on for another couple of months, she knew that Mike was already thinking ahead to their return to the US, when Star would begin work on her third album.

That reminded her of her earlier thoughts. "I really hope I'll get a chance to meet Athena Quincy at this funeral," she said. "And not just because it would be totally cool. I'd like to tell her how I was thinking about recording a cover of 'Star Bright.'"

Mike shot her a curious look. "You don't need her personal permission, darlin'," he said. "She recorded the most famous version, of course, but she didn't write the song and doesn't own the rights. And I'm already taking care of—"

"No, that's not what I mean," Star interrupted earnestly. She winced as Lola tugged at a knot in her curly blond hair, then continued. "I wouldn't feel right recording it unless she's cool with that, you know? Especially *that* song."

Understanding dawned in Mike's intelligent brown eyes. He shared a glance with Mags. "Gotcha," he said. "In that case, I'll try to make sure you and Athena get a chance to chat sometime over the next few days."

"Thanks." Star felt a ripple of nervousness in the pit of her stomach. Even though she was a celebrity now herself, she still got excited about meeting her own idols. And Athena Quincy was near the top of the list—Star had been listening to the famous diva's rich, strong, smoky voice for as long as she could remember. There was a reason Athena was known as the Empress of Entertainment; she was a living legend who had performed everywhere, from sold-out stadiums to the White House.

Star noticed that Lola was leaning back and staring at her with a pleased expression on her face. "There," Lola said. "You look as cute as a sack full of puppies, if I do say so myself."

"Good thing," Mike said, glancing out the window. "Looks like we're here."

He pushed away the newspaper, stood up, and hurried toward the front of the bus. Star leaned closer to the window. She watched as the bus eased to a stop at the curb in front of the colossal hotel where they would be staying, which took up a full city block.

"Hey," Star said. "There's nobody out there waiting for us."

"You mean nobody from hotel security is out there?" Mags sounded worried as she leaned toward the window too.

Star shook her head. "No, I mean nobody at all," she said. "Almost, anyway. Just a few people wandering past or whatever—no fans or paparazzi to be seen."

"Wow," Lola commented. "That's a change of pace for sure."

Star glanced forward at Mike and Tank, who appeared to be holding a slightly anxious conference as they peered out the bus's main door. Star stood up and walked toward them, followed by Lola, Mags, and Dudley. Mike glanced down at her, his brow furrowed and his expression slightly suspicious.

"Hold up a second, *Liebchen*," Tank told Star, flexing his impressive muscles as he glanced out the door at the empty sidewalk. "We're trying to figure out if something fishy's going on out there."

"Just let me call the head of hotel security." Mike was already dialing his cell phone. Hitting SEND, he held it to his ear, the toes of one of his purple cowboy boots tapping impatiently on the bus's carpeted floor. "Howdy, Mosley here," he said to whoever answered his call. "We're just outside your south entrance, and feelin' a little lonely. . . ."

He paused to listen. Star and Lola exchanged a curious glance. Star was used to being greeted by mobs of fans and reporters everywhere she went. Sometimes Mike joked that the paparazzi must have a homing device hidden on Dudley's collar or in one of the beads at the ends of Lola's dreadlocks, since they always seemed to know exactly where Star was going to turn up next.

A moment later Mike hung up and tucked his phone in his pocket. His expression had changed from anxious to amused. "Seems we lucked out," he said. "Eddie Urbane and his latest squeeze—you know, that tall, skinny blond; what's her name?"

"Xandra Om," Lola supplied. "She's that New Age guru turned wanna-be actress."

Mike nodded. "That's the one," he said. "Anyway, the two of 'em just arrived at the main entrance on the opposite side of the hotel. They're bein' swarmed even as we speak— apparently everyone who was waitin' for us got distracted by them. Hotel's sendin' a couple of guards over to help us in, but it looks like we won't need 'em."

Lola let out a snort. "Can't believe it," she commented. "Looks like that Urbane kid is actually turning out to be useful for once."

Star hid a smile. Nobody on her team liked seventeen-year-old rock star Eddie Urbane much, mostly thanks to the antics he'd pulled at the start of Star's tour to try to sabotage it. But Lola was the most outspoken about her distaste for the handsome young singer. That was really no surprise—Lola rarely kept her feelings about anything to herself, which got her in hot water from time to time.

A moment later a uniformed doorman pushed through

the heavy glass doors, flanked by a pair of burly security guards. "Okay, gang," Mike said. "Let's move."

Star clipped Dudley's leash onto his collar, then followed the adults as they stepped down out of the bus. It felt weird to exit the bus without being greeted by the deafening clamor of dozens or even hundreds of excited onlookers. She felt downright relaxed as she strolled across the wide sidewalk, and she could tell the rest of her team felt the same way. Unfortunately their mellow mood only lasted a moment before it was shattered by an excited squeal from nearby.

"Star! Star! There she is!"

"Omigod, it's really her!"

Glancing toward the sound of the shrieks, Star saw several girls around her own age rushing toward her at top speed. Star felt Tank immediately go tense beside her, while Mike spun on his heel to block her other side.

"It's okay, you guys," Star told the men quickly. "Looks like it's just a few fans. Guess they were the only ones loyal enough to stick around instead of running over to see Eddie. Can't we stop and talk to them for a second?"

She glanced up at Mike hopefully. Star loved meeting her fans, though it happened way too infrequently these days. In the very early days of her fame it had been a lot easier to answer their letters and e-mails, or chat with them after a show or other public appearance.

But then her first album, *Star Power*, had hit the top of the charts, and her debut video had gone into heavy rotation on PopTV. And just like that, her life had changed forever. These days she was lucky to catch a glimpse of her fans behind the crush of reporters that crowded around her outside every backstage door and lined both sides of every red carpet. Mike had hired someone to take care of the fan mail, which arrived in epic quantities every day of the year. Even when Star signed autographs at a music store or after a press conference, she usually didn't have more than a couple of seconds to say hello to each person there. That was one of the few things she would change about her life if she could, because she still remembered how it felt to be the fan on the other side of the bright lights, and how much it meant to those fans to get even the slightest attention from their favorite superstar.

Mike rubbed his mustache and sighed. But then he nodded. "S'pose that would be okay," he said. "But just for a second. Don't want to tempt fate here."

Star turned toward her fans, who had stopped at Tank's menacing look and were shuffling their feet uncertainly

15

about half a dozen yards away. "Hi," she called to them with a smile. "It's okay, you can come over here and say hello if you want."

The girls stepped forward, keeping a cautious eye on Tank. "Cheers," one of them said in a British accent. "Star Calloway? Is that really you?"

"It's really me," Star replied. "What are your names?"

The girls introduced themselves, a little shy at first, clearly awed by coming face-to-face with their idol. But Star had a talent for making everyone near her feel comfortable, and soon she and the British girls were chatting like old friends. Star did her best to answer a flurry of excited questions while autographing every scrap of paper the girls had in their purses and pockets. Dudley joined in the fun too, jumping up and down and barking until each of the girls had picked him up for a hug and received a tongue-bath from the friendly little dog. Star giggled as Dudley slurped one of the fans right across the lips.

"Oi!" the girl exclaimed, spitting and sputtering. "Quit that, Dudley, you devil. That's my favorite peach-flavored lip gloss, and I'm nearly out!"

"Dudsters loves peaches," Star said happily, handing back the bus pass she had just signed for another of the girls. "So, do any of you guys have dogs at home?"

"I do!" one of the girls replied, launching into a description of her own mischievous pet.

Star drank in every detail. She loved this. It was an incredible feeling to know that her music had made her friends all over the world. It was even more incredible to get to know some of them a bit as people—and to let them get to know her as someone beyond the pretty, blue-eyed face on the album cover or TV screen.

All too soon, though, she heard Mike clear his throat. "Hate to break this up, young ladies," he said, glancing around anxiously. "But I think we'd better skedaddle inside before someone else figures out we're here."

"Oh." Star couldn't help being disappointed. "Are you sure?"

"I'm sure."

Mike's tone was calm, but Star could tell from his expression that he was getting anxious. She nodded, knowing that he was right—it was better to get inside now, before someone spotted the tour bus or something. But knowing that didn't make it any easier to see the disappointed looks on her fans' faces at her manager's words.

"Sorry," Star told them. "I have to go. But it was mega-cool to meet you guys." She grinned, suddenly remembering the conversation on the bus earlier. "Oh, and don't forget—*carpe diem*!"

One of the girls answered, looking confused, but Star couldn't hear what she said over the sudden sound of shouting. Glancing over her shoulder, she saw a pack of reporters flying toward her, cameras held out before most of them like weapons. It would be only a matter of seconds before they reached her.

Vaguely aware that one of the hotel security guards was stepping forward to protect the British girls, Star allowed the other guards, along with Tank, to swoop her forward toward the open hotel door. She didn't dare look back as she ducked inside, the hotel doorman pulling the heavy glass doors shut behind her just in the nick of time.

Two

"... and it will be very exciting to see what this crop of young talents will do next," Ernie Golden said in his deep, raspy voice on the TV screen. "Eddie Urbane, Star Calloway, maybe a few others . . . they are the future of music. A bright future."

Star gasped, sitting up a little straighter on the sofa. She was watching a PopTV retrospective on Golden's long career. Some of the footage was familiar—his acceptance speeches at various awards shows, the talk he'd given at Athena Quincy's fiftieth-birthday tribute concert a few years back— but she'd never seen this particular interview with the late producer before.

"Wow," she murmured, feeling flattered at Golden's kind words. "I can't believe he mentioned me like that. That's so cool!"

"There you are, babydoll." Lola bustled into the room. "It's about time to start getting ready for tonight. We only have an hour before we're supposed to head downstairs."

Star blinked and looked up at her. "Oh, okay," she said. "This is the welcome party thing, right?"

It had been several hours since Star and her team had checked into their large, luxurious hotel suite. Mike was on the phone in another room, Tank had gone downstairs to check out the hotel gym, and Mags was busy with some paperwork. That had given Star an unusual hour or two of free time. She had finished the latest homework assignments Mags had given her, and now she was lounging on the hotel suite's plush velvet sofa watching TV with Dudley snoozing on her lap.

Star gently shoved the sleeping dog aside. He snorted and snuffled but didn't wake up, instead snuggling against the soft fabric of the sofa cushion while a trail of drool slipped out of the corner of his mouth.

"Okay," Star said, standing up. "So, what am I going to wear tonight?"

Before Lola could answer, there was a knock on the door. "That must be room service," Lola said, hurrying to answer.

"Room service?" Star trailed behind the stylist, feeling confused. "Why? I thought you just said we were supposed to leave for this party in like an hour."

"We are." Lola swung the door open. A hotel employee, a

young woman with wavy brown hair, was standing outside with a cart loaded with covered trays. The employee shot Star a shy sidelong glance as she wheeled the cart into the room.

"Thank you," Star told her.

The young woman bowed slightly, looking rather awed. "You're quite welcome, Miss Calloway," she said breathlessly. "Shall I set up the table for you?"

"No thanks," Lola said pleasantly, reaching into the star-shaped petty cash box by the door and handing the woman a tip. "We'll take it from here."

Once the employee was gone, Star stepped forward to peek at the food beneath the gleaming stainless-steel covers. The trays held all sorts of dishes, from pasta to salad. There was even a plate full of cookies and pastries for dessert.

"Maybe I'm missing something here," she said, her mouth watering as she looked over the large selection of pastries and wondered if Mike and Mags would let her eat dessert first for once. "But what's the point of this party if we're stuffing ourselves before we go?"

Lola chuckled as she started to clear the table of the papers, keys, and other miscellaneous items the others had dropped there upon their arrival. "Good question, sugar," she said. "It does seem a little crazy, doesn't it? Kind of like my nutty old

Aunt Esther, who always used to clean her house before the cleaning lady came . . ."

Mike wandered in just in time to hear the last part of the conversation. "Very funny," he told Lola dryly. Then he glanced at Star. "They're callin' this thing tonight a party, but I'm afraid it's going to be more work than play for you, darlin'. It's an excuse to get all the celebrity attendees together and give the press a chance to take some pictures of y'all. That keeps them happy so they're less likely to get in the way at the show tomorrow night or the funeral itself the day after. Get it?"

"Totally," Star said with a slight sigh. She knew she shouldn't be surprised; if a funeral could turn into a media extravaganza, it almost made sense that a pre-funeral party could become nothing more than a publicity event. "So I'm not going to this thing to eat or hang out. I'm going to mingle and be seen."

Mike smiled at her. "You got it," he said. "So better fill up now. Why don't you go gather the troops while Lola and I set up here?"

As the adults transferred the food from the cart to the table, Star hurried off to find Tank and Mags. Soon all five of them were tucking in.

Over the Top

"Okay, babydoll," Lola said, glancing at Star over a forkful of salad. "So what do you feel like wearing tonight—the pink-and-white outfit, your blue chiffon skirt with the beaded top from that designer you like, or that cute new strappy silver dress we picked up in Amsterdam?"

A little over an hour later Star stood patiently in a hallway of the hotel while Lola adjusted the complicated straps of her shimmering silver dress and its matching sandals. "There," the stylist said at last, stepping back with a satisfied smile. "You and that dress are going to photograph like a dream. Just don't move your shoulders around too much, and everything should stay where it's supposed to."

"Thanks." Star smiled at her, then glanced up at Mike, who was standing by along with Tank. "Should we head in?"

"Let's do it."

Star took a deep breath, then stepped forward as Tank swung open the door to the hotel's fanciest ballroom. She was greeted with the blinding glare of dozens of camera flashes, along with a clamor of excited voices.

"Star! Star! Over here!"

"Star, sweetheart—a smile this way, please!"

"Star! Yo, Star! How's the tour going?"

"This way, Star! Turn to the left!"

Even though she could hardly see where she was going in the bright explosion of flashes, Star stepped forward and spun on her heel, smiling and waving. She was careful to keep her blue eyes wide open and not squint. She wasn't the least bit shy or retiring, but at first she had found it a little scary to face the howl of an eager press corps. But by now she was used to it. Besides, she was aware of Mike, Tank, and Lola standing protectively just a few feet behind her, not to mention the hotel's security guards, who were enforcing the velvet ropes separating the reporters from the red-carpeted pathway leading into the main part of the ballroom.

"Good evening, everyone!" Star called out over the clamor as she waved again, resisting the urge to scratch her nose, which had suddenly started itching, or to check the straps on her dress to make sure they weren't falling. "It's such an honor to be here to celebrate Mr. Golden's life."

"Did you ever work with Golden, Star?" a reporter shouted.

Star turned in the general direction of the questioner, though she wasn't sure exactly which reporter that was. "Unfortunately no," she said. "I never got the chance to work with him. I wish I could have."

"How's your tour going, Star?" another reporter yelled

from the back of the pack. "Are you going to be playing any dates back in the US this year?"

Star winced. It seemed strange to be answering questions about herself when this event was supposed to be all about Ernie Golden. But she answered politely. "It's going very well, and it's oodles of fun," she said. "We're off to Ireland in a few days, then France, and then we'll be moving on to Asia pretty soon after that. We've only got a few dates scheduled back home in October, but we may add more later in the fall."

"Any word on your missing family, Star?" someone else called out.

"Not lately," Star replied. "But we're staying hopeful."

She stood there for a few more minutes answering question after question. A few involved Ernie Golden, but the rest were the usual queries about the tour, Star's latest chart-topping hit, the commercial she'd just shot, and similar topics. Star answered them all as patiently as she could—that was part of her job, after all. Still, she couldn't help wishing some of the reporters seemed a little more interested in the reason they were all there.

Finally, as a British TV star entered to distract the reporters, Star and her team were able to make it past the door. They headed into the hotel ballroom, where the party was in full swing. Looking around, Star spotted countless famous faces, including a cute teen guy with sleek brown hair standing near the bar at the far end of the room.

"Hey, check it out," she said. "There's Ky." She waved vigorously at Kynan Kane, the lead singer of the boy band Boysterous. Star had met her fellow American teen pop idol on several occasions, and always enjoyed Ky's outgoing personality and great sense of humor.

"Run on over and say hi if you want," Mike told her. "We'll catch up with you in a sec."

"Cool," Star said. "Thanks."

She tossed him a grateful smile before starting across the crowded room. Mike rarely let her go anywhere in public without either himself or Tank right at her side—it just wasn't safe most of the time. But this party was closed to the public, and the reporters and photographers circulating through the room appeared to be mostly the ones Mike referred to as "the pros" rather than "the vultures," which was one of his more polite names for the pushiest paparazzi.

"Star! Is that you?"

Halfway across the room Star turned to see a moon-faced woman in her thirties hurrying toward her, a broad smile on her heavily made-up face. She recognized the woman as

April Dawn, a sitcom actress who had just released her first country music album to overwhelming critical indifference.

"Hello," Star said politely, smiling at the woman. "Nice to see you again, Ms. Dawn."

"Oh, Star!" April cried breathlessly, her enormous, poufed blond hairdo quivering along with her fuchsia-painted lower lip. "Isn't this party just incredible? I'm so happy I could come; but then again, how could I miss it? The Golden Ear was just so great, don't you think? And now that I'm a musician myself, I wanted to pay my respects, and . . ."

Star kept her smile steady as the woman chattered at her nonstop about Ernie Golden, music, the local weather, and recent events in her own life. Star had only met April in passing at an awards show the past winter, though from the way the woman was talking at the moment, no one ever would have guessed they were anything but long-separated best friends.

"'Scuse me," Mike said, suddenly appearing out of the crowd and breaking into the woman's monologue. He put a hand on Star's shoulder, meanwhile shooting April his most charming smile and slipping deeper into a Texas twang. "Ah'm afraid I gotta pull our Star away for a sec—hope y'all can forgive me."

"Oh! Of course." April looked disappointed, but smiled agreeably. Then her eyes lit up as she spotted someone over Star's shoulder. "Kynan! Darling! Is that you?"

Star sighed as the woman rushed away. "Thanks," she murmured to Mike. She didn't say anything more, all too aware of the reporters lurking here and there throughout the room.

But Mike understood perfectly. "Sure thing, sweetheart," he murmured back with a wink. "Guess you can say hello to Ky later, hmm? Looks like he's going to be busy for a while."

For the next few minutes Star worked her way through the crowd, greeting people she knew and being introduced to those she didn't. She lost count of how many times photographers stopped her to take her picture, or followed her around shooting video of her chatting with the other guests.

She noticed with a twinge of pride that Mike seemed to know just about everyone in the room—and everyone seemed to want to say hello to him. She was watching her manager chat with a trio of record executives in business suits when Tank approached holding a glass of soda. "Here you go, Star-baby," he said, handing it to her. "Thought you might be getting thirsty, what with all that smiling."

"Thanks, Tank," Star said gratefully. "I really needed th—"

"Tank!" A female voice interrupted her. "Tank Massimo! Is that really you?"

For a second Star feared the speaker was April Dawn, back to corral yet another of her long-lost best friends. Instead, when she turned to look she saw a pretty thirtyish woman dressed in a black pantsuit, with a mass of curly black hair falling over her slender shoulders and an intelligent sparkle in her brown eyes.

"Anita?" Tank exclaimed. "Am I seeing things? *Dios mío!* How long has it been?"

The two adults started chattering excitedly at each other, at least half of it in Spanish. Star sipped her soda, waiting politely for as long as she could stand it. Then she cleared her throat.

"Excuse me," she said playfully. "Hey, Tank, I'm still here, remember?"

"Oh!" Tank's broad, tanned face turned red. "Sorry, Star-baby. This is an old friend, Anita Martinez. Anita, you probably recognize Star Calloway."

"Of course." Anita held out her hand with a warm smile. "It's so nice to meet you. I'm a big fan."

"Thanks." Star smiled back as she shook Anita's hand,

liking Tank's friend immediately. "So how do you and Tank know each other?"

Anita laughed, tossing her hair back over one shoulder. "Oh, we've been bumping into each other forever," she said, giving Tank's muscular arm a playful punch. "Isn't that right, big guy?" She smiled at Star. "I'm a studio musician—bass and keyboards, mostly."

"Don't be modest," Tank broke in. "Anita here can play the heck out of just about every instrument ever invented."

"Really? That's so cool!" Star smiled again at Anita, but she was also watching Tank out of the corner of her eye. Was she imagining things, or had Anita's appearance brought an extra sparkle to her bodyguard's brown eyes?

Ooh, I wonder if maybe there's more to this so-called friendship than they're letting on, Star thought. *Maybe Tank has always had a crush on Anita or something; maybe she's some kind of unrequited love. . . .*

She realized she knew next to nothing about Tank's romantic life. All she knew was that for the past two years since becoming her driver, personal trainer, and head bodyguard, he'd been too busy to do much dating. And that on the rare occasion someone set him up with a woman, it never seemed to last long.

"So is any of the rest of the old studio gang here tonight?" Tank asked Anita.

The woman nodded. "Tons," she said. "I was just talking to Janine and Stewie over there. . . ." She gestured vaguely toward a cluster of people in the center of the room.

"Why don't you and Anita go over and say hi?" Star suggested brightly, suddenly very interested to see what might happen if Tank and his pretty young friend spent a little more time together. "I'll be okay here with Mike and Lola." She gestured toward the other two adults, who were still chatting with the record executives nearby.

Tank looked uncertain. "Are you sure?" he said. "Maybe I'd better check in with Mike first. . . ."

He headed over and spoke to Mike. It was too noisy in the room for Star to hear what they were saying, though she saw Mike turn and glance at Anita. Then he nodded.

"Okay," Tank said, returning to Star. "Stick close to Mike or Lola, all right? I'll be back soon."

"No problem," Star said. "Nice meeting you, Anita."

"Same here," the woman said. "And thanks for letting me steal Tank for a while, Star. I'm sure I'll see you around."

Star watched the two of them hurry away as she sipped her soda and enjoyed the rare moment of peace. When Tank and

Anita disappeared in the crowd, she glanced around, wondering who else had arrived while she wasn't looking.

I wonder if Jade is here yet, she thought, hiking up one of the straps of her dress. *I really want to make sure to say hi to her tonight.*

Jade was another young singer, just a year or so older than Star. At first Star had hoped the two of them would become good friends as soon as they met—after all, who else could understand her crazy life better than someone else who was living it too? But they had started off on the wrong foot when a reporter had misquoted Star in the newspaper, making it sound as if she had insulted Jade. Jade's manager, an unpleasant man named Stan Starkey, had retaliated by launching a media war, which had ended with Jade revealing Star's parents' disappearance, which had been a secret from most of the world until then. The two girls had taken tentative steps toward conciliation since that time, though Starkey seemed determined to remain as hateful as possible toward Star and her whole team.

Still, Star wasn't giving up on Jade. She suspected that there was an interesting, sensitive, creative person in there, if she could just get past Jade's suspicious attitude—not to mention her obnoxious manager.

There was no sign of Jade, but Star did spot Kynan Kane standing alone near the bar. After giving Mike a wave to let him know where she was going, she hurried over to finally say hello.

As Star and Ky were catching up a few minutes later, a sudden tremor of excitement ran through the room like an electric current. A reporter rushed past, muttering urgently into his cell phone: "They're here! They're here!"

Star glanced curiously toward the entrance. "Wonder who that is."

"Must be, like, the President of England, dude," Ky joked. "Who else would cause such a buzz?"

Star rolled her eyes and giggled. She knew Ky was perfectly aware that there was no such thing as a President of England. It was just part of his act—in his band, his role was the good-looking bad boy who didn't care about anything except girls and cars.

"Very funny," she said, poking him in the shoulder. "Seriously, though. I wonder if it's Athena Quincy—she hasn't showed yet. I don't think Jade is here either."

Ky shrugged. "Athena, maybe," he said. "Jade, no way. She might have one hit album, but she's not hot enough to get that kind of action here."

Star winced slightly, a little shocked as always by the cold-hearted calculations of the entertainment world. Still, she suspected Ky was right. Jade's career was definitely on the way up, but in a room full of heavy hitters she was practically B-list.

Before Star could wonder any longer, a loud shout went up from the group of reporters gathered near the door, which was growing every second. The door swung open, and a tall, handsome, dark-haired guy in his late teens slouched through with a pretty, slender young blond woman hanging on his arm.

"Oh," Star said as the flashes exploded. "It's Eddie and his new girlfriend."

"Xandra Om," Ky supplied, taking a step toward the newcomers and staring curiously. "Yo, she definitely has her cute on tonight! No wonder Eddie was willing to follow her off to Tibet or wherever."

Star watched the pair with interest as they stopped to face the reporters. Eddie was dressed in a stylish charcoal gray suit, his collar and tie slightly rumpled to match his perpetually rumpled dark hair, while his companion wore a gauzy two-piece outfit made of shimmering gold fabric. Star didn't know much about Xandra Om other than what she'd read in the tabloids. Xandra had first come to public attention as the host of a short-lived New Age TV show and the author of its companion book, *Embrace Your Spirit*. She'd been romantically linked with several musicians and Hollywood leading men before her latest romance with Eddie Urbane.

While the reporters yelled out questions, Xandra suddenly flipped her long blond hair over her shoulders and took a step forward, disappearing from Star's sight behind a cluster of reporters. A second later an excited howl went up from the press and other onlookers, and the cameras flashed more furiously than ever.

"What's going on?" Star cried, standing on tiptoes to try to get a better view. But at just four foot nine, all she could see were the backs of the people rushing from all over the room to find out what was happening.

Ky didn't hesitate. He leaped onto the nearby bar, ignoring startled looks from the bartenders. "Yo!" he exclaimed with a laugh. "Check it out, Star. She just lifted up her top—she's got a picture of Ernie Golden painted on her stomach! At least I think that's who it's supposed to be. . . ."

Star shook her head, amused. "Wow," she commented. "I never thought it would happen."

"What?" Ky asked, his gaze still glued on Xandra.

Star giggled. "Eddie finally found a girlfriend who's just as wild and publicity-crazy as he is. They're the perfect couple!"

Three

A few minutes later Ky's manager appeared and dragged him off to meet someone. Eddie and Xandra had finally made it past the press into the main part of the room, and Star headed toward them to say hello.

I don't know why I bother, she told herself as she weaved her way through the crowd, yanking at her dress strap, which seemed determined to flop off her shoulder. *If he even acknowledges me at all, it'll probably just be because he knows the reporters are watching us . . . especially after those rumors he started a while back about the two of us being a couple.*

She smiled slightly. Maybe Lola's suspicions of the good-looking young singer were rubbing off on her at last.

No, she told herself as she dodged a pair of American TV actors hamming it up in front of a reporter's video camera. *I'm just getting a little smarter about people, I guess. I mean, I know Eddie's kind of a rat. But he's not all bad—nobody is. Besides, I'm sort of grateful to him for flying me back to the US that time, even if he had ulterior motives. And I still like his music. . . .*

By then she had reached the couple. Eddie and Xandra were standing side-by-side talking to a man Star didn't recognize. When Eddie noticed Star standing there, he looked underwhelmed.

"Oh," he said as the other man melted away into the crowd. "Hi."

Star ignored his lack of enthusiasm. "Hi, Eddie," she said. "Good to see you again. Isn't this party all kinds of cool? It's nice that everyone is here to pay their respects to Ernie the Ear."

"Yeah." Eddie pursed his lips. "That's exactly why I'm here."

Xandra nudged at his arm. "Eddie, aren't you going to introduce me?" she asked, smiling at Star. Without waiting for him to respond, she stepped forward and took Star by the hand. "It's so uplifting to meet you, Star," she said. "I'm Xandra."

"Yes, I know," Star said, doing her best to shake the young woman's hand, even though it lay in her own like a dead fish. Up close Xandra was even more striking than in photos, with her chiseled cheekbones and her intense green eyes flecked with gold. "Um, I've never seen your show or anything, but . . ."

She trailed off as Xandra let out a dramatic gasp, her grip suddenly tightening on Star's hand. "Oh!" Xandra cried.

"Star, I—listen, I'm a little bit psychic, and I'm getting a really strong spirit vision from you right now. An important message . . ."

Whatever else she was going to say was drowned out by a sudden explosive uproar from the entrance. Glancing over, Star saw that the door had just opened again, though the crowd prevented her from seeing who was coming in.

Just then a pair of reporters raced by, one carrying a microphone and the other a video camera. "It's Athena! It's Athena!" the microphone-carrying one cried out breathlessly. "We have to get this! Hurry!"

If Eddie and Xandra's arrival had caused an explosion of interest, Athena Quincy's caused a meltdown. People from all over the room moved in her direction as if they were being pulled by a magnet. It seemed that everyone wanted a glimpse of the Empress of Entertainment.

Star bit her lip, wishing that she could be as tall as Mike so she could see over everyone's heads. She had barely finished the thought when Athena's bodyguards, famous throughout the industry for their efficiency as well as their unusual white uniforms and cool taciturnity, moved out into the crowd, firmly pushing back the spectators into several orderly groups. That allowed Star to see that the famous diva hadn't actually entered yet, and it also showed her an opening in the crowd. She hurried forward and found a spot between a photographer and a well-known entertainment reporter. The photographer didn't spare her a second glance as she took photo after photo, though the reporter did a double take when he recognized Star standing beside him. But his attention was diverted when the door opened again and Athena Quincy entered.

Athena strode into the party like a queen stepping into her throne room. She was dressed in a brilliant emerald green gown that turned her ample frame into an impressive spectacle, and her glistening black hair was piled into an elaborate do atop her head. A dash of iridescent green powder highlighted her amber eyes and mahogany skin.

"Good evening, everyone." Athena's regal voice carried easily over the murmurs of the crowd, sounding nearly as rich and melodious as it did when she was singing. "It's so wonderful to see such an outpouring of love here for my dear friend Ernie. He would have adored this party—so let's all enjoy it in his memory. *Carpe diem!* Thank you all for coming!"

"Athena! Athena! Over here!"

Several dozen voices rose out of the crowd, clamoring for the Empress's attention. Star allowed herself to be shuffled back by the excited reporters until she was once again standing with Eddie and Xandra.

"Gee, let me guess," Eddie commented sarcastically. "Athena's here?"

"Bingo," Star replied absently, still craning her neck for another glimpse.

Eddie let out a snort. "Don't know why everyone's acting like she's the freakin' queen of the world," he muttered. "She hasn't had a hit song in like three years."

Star glanced at him, a bit irritated by his comment. "Duh," she said, hiking up her loose dress strap again. "She hasn't released a new album in three years either. So how's she supposed to have a hit song?"

Xandra laughed. "She's got you there, Eddie," she said, winking at Star.

Star smiled back, pleased and a bit surprised that Xandra was backing her up. "Besides," she told Eddie, "you have to remember, Athena's been making hit songs since before any of us were born. She's a legend—she totally deserves this kind of acclaim and stuff."

"Whatever." Eddie rolled his eyes. "Looks like I'm out-voted."

"Sorry, love." Xandra gave him a quick peck on the cheek,

then turned toward Star again. "Listen," she said. "As I was saying before, I need to talk to you about this vision I just had when we met. I think it's really—"

"Star! There you are, darlin'." Mike suddenly appeared at Star's side, sounding breathless. "Been lookin' all over for you. Want to come over and say howdy to Athena?"

Star gulped, a whole flock of butterflies suddenly taking flight and spinning around frantically in her stomach. Glancing around, she saw that Athena, flanked by several of her white-uniformed bodyguards, was making her way deeper into the ballroom. People were still clustering around her, and not just reporters and photographers, but the other celebrity guests as well, many of them legendary idols in their own right.

"O-okay," Star said, trying to hold down her sudden attack of nerves. Star rarely got nervous about anything— she could stand in front of a sold-out stadium at one of her concerts without breaking a sweat. But this was different. This was Athena, the Empress of Entertainment, the first singer Star had ever known and admired, the favorite of her whole family. Star briefly closed her eyes and touched her star necklace, wishing her parents could be there to share this exciting moment.

Then, with an apologetic smile for Eddie and Xandra, she followed her manager off through the crowd. When they neared Athena, one of her bodyguards held up a hand to stop them, but Athena looked over and spotted Mike.

"Why, it's Mike Mosley! Darling!" she exclaimed, shooing the bodyguard aside as she rushed over to Mike, the folds of her emerald green dress gusting out behind her. "How wonderful to see you!"

"Right back atcha, Miz Quincy," Mike responded with a tip of an imaginary cowboy hat. "Always a pleasure."

Athena grabbed him and planted a kiss on each of his cheeks, leaving a shadow of lipstick on either side of his bushy mustache. "Don't be so formal, Mike," she scolded. "You know you don't have to call me Ms. Quincy. 'O Great Exalted One' will be just fine."

With that, the diva turned and winked playfully at Star. Star giggled despite her shyness.

"Now, who have we here?" Athena said, smiling at Star. "Let me guess—this is your lovely young protégé, Miss Star Calloway. It's my pleasure to meet you at last, my dear. I've been following your career with great interest."

Star was so overwhelmed at Athena's words that it took her

a moment to find her voice to answer. "Th-thank you, Ms. Quincy," she stammered at last, shaking the diva's outstretched hand and almost scraping her finger on one of Athena's large bejeweled rings. "It's totally an honor to meet you. I've been your biggest fan since I was born. Before I was born, actually—my mother listened to your albums the whole time she was pregnant!"

Athena threw back her head and laughed out loud. "How marvelous!" she cried. "Star, you're a delight—just like your music. I have to tell you, I simply adore the song you've been performing on tour, 'Over the Top.' Please tell me you're planning to include it on your next album."

Star blushed. She was used to hearing all kinds of people praise her songs, from reviewers and record executives to fans and other artists. But hearing Athena Quincy compliment her was different somehow. Special.

"Yes, we are," she said. "Thank you." Somehow, the words didn't seem meaningful enough. She wanted to express to Athena how grateful she was for her graciousness, how incredible it was to meet her at last . . .

Before she could come up with the right words, a well-known American anchorman turned up with a camera crew wanting to talk with the Empress. With one last smile for Star and Mike, Athena turned away to answer his questions.

"Well?" Mike glanced down at Star as they stepped away. "Happy now?"

"Athena was so great!" Star sighed happily as she touched her necklace. "Too bad I didn't get a chance to mention 'Star Bright' to her." She shrugged. "Although, I don't know— even though she was so mega-nice, I'm really not sure I have the guts to talk to her about it after all."

Mike chuckled. "She is pretty impressive, isn't she?" he said, his gaze wandering over toward where Athena was holding court. "It's no surprise they call her the Empress."

At that moment there was a slightly more subdued shout of excitement from the entrance. Glancing over, Star spotted Jade entering the room. Jade was wearing an edgily stylish red dress, her long, silky dark hair pulled up into glossy tendrils. Right behind her was a stocky man wearing a magenta suit and an unpleasant expression—her manager, Stan Starkey. His assistant, a pale, twitchy young woman named Manda, was there too, looking even gaunter than usual in a clingy black evening gown.

Star wrinkled her nose slightly at the sight of Starkey and

Manda. While she always tried to see the best in everyone, it was hard to find anything at all to like in those two. She often wondered how Jade stood it.

"Jade just got here," she told Mike. "Is it okay if I go over and say hi?"

"Sure, sweetheart," Mike said. "Just give a shout if you need me."

Star nodded. As her manager hurried off toward another part of the room, she turned and headed toward the door, where Jade was still talking to the press. She had only gone a few steps when she felt someone grab her arm. Tensing immediately for an encounter with a pushy reporter, she spun around and instead found herself face-to-face with Xandra.

"Oh," Star said, going limp with relief. She saw Eddie standing behind his girlfriend looking bored. "It's you guys. I was just on my way to—"

"I can't wait any longer to talk to you about this!" Xandra cried dramatically. "It's too important!"

"What?" Star said, startled and a bit embarrassed. Xandra's voice was loud enough to carry well beyond their little group of three. Out of the corner of her eye, Star could see several nearby reporters turning curiously to see what was going on. "Xandra, I—"

Once again the young woman interrupted her. "Star," she exclaimed, grabbing her by the hand. "Listen to me. I'm getting a strong vision of your missing family!"

Four

Star gasped, startled by Xandra's announcement. "Wh-what?" she blurted out. "What are you talking about?"

Xandra kept her gold-flecked eyes trained on Star's face. "It's in your aura," she said. "It's very strong, though not entirely clear. . . ."

Noticing that more reporters were starting to take notice of them, Star grabbed Xandra by the arm. "Come on, let's go talk about this somewhere more private, okay?" she urged.

"Oh, but we can talk about it right here!" Xandra said. "I don't want to lose this moment—your aura is shimmering, and the images are crying out to me. . . ." She swayed slightly, her eyes half closing. "Please, they are crying to be heard, Star! I—I think it's your mother calling out to me the loudest. . . ."

Star bit her lip. She really didn't believe in ESP or auras or any of the rest of that sort of thing, but she couldn't help being curious about whatever Xandra thought she was sensing. Still, that didn't mean she wanted to turn up in the tabloids the next day with a headline like STAR CONSULTS THE STARS FOR GUIDANCE or MISSING CALLOWAY FAMILY MAKES CONTACT THROUGH BLOND BEAUTY. Even her head publicist, who loved almost any kind of publicity or media exposure, would be horrified by that sort of thing.

"Come on," she said more firmly, tugging at Xandra's arm. "We can totally talk more about this. *Privately.*"

"Oh, just go with her, already, Xan," Eddie put in, sounding impatient. Without waiting for a response, he turned and stalked off in the direction of the bar. "I'm going to get a soda," he added over his shoulder.

Xandra shrugged and sighed. "All right, Star," she said patiently. "I suppose if you're not spiritually comfortable talking about this here . . ."

"Thank you." Pushing her way past the reporters, who watched curiously but didn't try to follow, Star led the way to a quiet corner of the ballroom behind some large potted palms. Once she was sure they were out of earshot of the party crowd, she turned to face Xandra. "Now," she said, "what are you trying to tell me?"

Xandra took her firmly by both hands, her grip not the least bit fishlike now. "It's your aura, Star," she said. "As I was trying to tell you before. It's telling me that your family is almost ready to be found."

Star gulped, surprised at how hard the words hit her but trying not to show it. "What was that about my mother?" she asked, her hand itching to touch her necklace. But Xandra was still holding both her hands tightly, so Star resisted the urge.

Xandra rolled her eyes up toward the ceiling, her pretty face taking on an oddly vacant expression. "It's rather fuzzy, I'm afraid," she intoned in a calm, peaceful voice. "First of all, she wants you to know that she and your father and brother are safe and happy, but that they miss you. There's something about water, and waves . . ." Suddenly she blinked, glancing down at Star. "Oh," she added. "I'm sorry, Star. I just lost the connection again. But I'm sure if we spent more time together over the next few days, I could figure out more of your family's message. I'm very sensitive to psychic phenomena of all kinds."

"Really?" Star said politely, mostly just to buy time to figure out what she thought of Xandra's words.

"Oh, yes!" Xandra replied. "A couple of years ago when I met Harold Harrington—of course you know who he is, the great British actor—I helped him receive a message from his recently departed father, and . . ."

She rambled on, describing more of her psychic experiences over the years. But Star wasn't really listening.

She can't be for real, she told herself. *Can she? I mean, it's fun to think that there might be such a thing as ESP or whatever. But there's no way my family could really be sending me some kind of psychic message. . . .*

". . . and so I really think we need to spend as much time as possible together," Xandra said urgently.

"Oh, um, what?" Star blurted out, realizing that the woman had moved on from talking about herself to talking about Star again.

"I can be there anytime you need me," Xandra said. "I'd be happy to join you for meals, tag along on interviews, go shopping, sit with you at the funeral—anything you like. That way I won't miss any important opportunities to read you. And maybe together we can find your family at last!"

"Hmm." Suddenly Star was getting an image of her own—an image of Eddie Urbane shadowing her for the next couple of days along with his girlfriend. Was this another of Eddie's plots to gain himself some extra publicity? That seemed a lot more likely than anything Xandra was saying.

"We could start tomorrow," Xandra continued, not

seeming to notice Star's skeptical expression. "Eddie and I are throwing a lunch reception for a few selected guests at an adorable little local restaurant just around the corner. Would you like to come as my special guest?"

Star hesitated. She knew she should probably say thanks, but no thanks. After all, she had fallen for way too many of Eddie's publicity stunts before. For all she knew, Eddie had convinced his girlfriend to lure Star to that restaurant so he could use her presence as yet another photo op for himself.

But how do I know it's not true? A little voice popped into her head all of a sudden. *How do I know she's not really getting some kind of message from my family? Stranger things have happened, right?*

She knew she was grasping at straws by even entertaining the thought. Still, she couldn't quite resist the possibility, however slight. Hadn't she vowed to do anything she could to bring her family home again? Besides, it wouldn't do any harm if she did wind up in a few more photos with Eddie. It wasn't as if both of them weren't already getting plenty of extra exposure just by attending Golden's funeral extravaganza . . . Thinking about Ernie Golden made her remember his trademark phrase: *carpe diem.*

"All right," she told Xandra impulsively. "I'll ask my manager. If he okays it, I guess I could come to the lunch tomorrow and we'll see what happens."

"Fabulous!" Xandra said, looking pleased. "I'm sure we'll be able to reach a breakthrough if we both stay really open and accepting."

Star still wasn't feeling quite so sure. But she shrugged. "Come on," she said. "I'd better get back to the party before my people notice I'm missing and panic."

The two of them headed back to the main part of the room. As they passed a group of mostly older, less glamorously dressed men and women on the outskirts of the party, Star noticed Stan Starkey talking intently to a portly man in a business suit.

". . . and I can have her ready to perform any song you choose by tomorrow night. You'd be a fool not to take advantage of this offer," Starkey was saying as Star passed within earshot. He seemed to be going for a tone of jovial persuasion, but it came out sounding more like a threat. "Jade's on her way up, and Athena could only benefit from an association with the youth culture. Got to keep up with the times, you know, if you want to keep those discs outta the bargain bins . . ."

Star shook her head slightly as she kept walking, soon moving out of earshot. It sounded as though Starkey was trying to wheedle Jade's way onto the program of the next night's event. Then she realized that although Manda had been buzzing around just behind Starkey's shoulder as usual, Jade herself hadn't been anywhere in sight. That meant that she was free of her obnoxious management for a change.

Deciding to take advantage of that rare opportunity, Star excused herself from Xandra and immediately began scanning the room. She soon spotted Jade standing at the far end of the room near a large poster of Ernie Golden. She was talking to a skinny young male reporter and looking bored.

Star hurried over. "Sorry to interrupt," she said brightly. "Jade, I just wanted to come over and say hi."

Jade tossed her head to flip a tendril out of her eyes. "Hey, Star," she said with a small but sincere-looking smile. She glanced at the reporter. "Sorry, gotta go," she said. "Star and I need to catch up."

"But Jade, I wanted to ask you about . . ."

"Sorry," Jade said, cutting off the rest of the reporter's sentence brusquely. "I said I have to go, okay?"

The reporter shrugged. "Whatever," he muttered, jotting a note on his pad. A well-known PopTV VJ wandered past at that moment, and the reporter's eyes lit up. "Excuse me, Mr. Bash? I just want to ask you a few questions . . ."

When he was gone, Jade sighed so hard that several of her tendrils blew outward. "I hate these stupid events," she said.

Star smiled sympathetically. "I know, they're kind of a pain," she said. "I'd much rather spend my time talking to real fans or something, instead of reporters."

"I guess." Jade sounded unconvinced. "If you ask me, fans are a pain most of the time too. They always act like you should be all kinds of thrilled to see them. I mean, it's not like I don't go through that like a million times a day, okay?"

"I see what you mean," Star said thoughtfully, pushing at her pesky dress strap. "But look at it this way. We may get fans coming up to us on the street all the time, right? But to each of those fans, it's the only time they've ever run into us. You know? Like, in their world it's a once-in-a-lifetime event or whatever—they probably can't even imagine that it might be different for us."

Jade shrugged. "Never thought of it that way," she said. "Guess I'll try to remember that next time or whatever. But it's still a pain." She glanced around the room. "Anyway, thanks for coming over. You totally saved me from even more of that guy's mad boring questions."

"You're welcome." Star smiled, noting that the other girl's voice sounded as friendly as she'd ever heard it. "So this is some funeral, huh? Are you going to the remembrance concert thing tomorrow night?"

"Guess so," Jade said. "You?"

Star nodded. "Hey," she said impulsively. "Want to sit together? I'm sure my manager wouldn't mind."

Jade looked surprised but pleased. "That sounds okay," she said. "I'll have to ask Stan, though. He's still trying to get me on the bill doing, like, some kind of duet or something with Athena Quincy." She rolled her eyes. "Uh-huh, like maybe that would happen—on the planet Oh Yeah Right."

Star giggled. "Hey, you never know."

"Anyway," Jade went on, tugging at the hem of her short dress, "he's not that crazy about you, in case you didn't notice. So he might try to force me to sit with someone else." She grimaced. "He keeps trying to get me to, like, buddy up to some of the other big stars at this thing. Especially the hot young male ones like Kynan Kane and Eddie Urbane. Gee, you think he's trying to get me a date 'cuz he's worried that I'm lonely?"

Her voice dripped with so much sarcasm that Star gulped slightly before forcing a smile. Every time she encountered

Jade, she seemed less happy with her manager. Star wished there was something she could do to help the other young star, though she wasn't sure what that might be, other than continuing to offer her friendship.

Star glanced around, biting her lip. "I hope I'm not going to get you in trouble by talking to you like this," she said. "I mean, I knew Mr. Starkey wasn't crazy about Mike or me, but . . ."

"Don't worry about it." Jade waved one hand lazily. "Stan can't tell me who to talk to, okay? I'll deal with him if he squawks."

"Cool." Star was relieved that Jade didn't sound worried. In fact, she almost seemed as if she would welcome the chance to stand up to Starkey. Star glanced up as a good-looking young man in a tuxedo walked by. "Hey," she hissed, poking Jade in the arm. "How about that guy? Think your manager would approve him?"

Jade glanced over. "Nope," she said. "Not famous enough. Any potential friend or boyfriend needs to have at least one platinum record or hit TV show or movie, okay?" She grinned. "Too bad Stan thinks you're so bunk; otherwise you'd be perfect!"

Star giggled. "Oh, well," she said. "I can introduce you to

Ky or Eddie if you want, but I've got to warn you, I'm not sure either one is good boyfriend material."

"Really?" Jade sounded curious. "Spill it. What's their deal?"

"Oh, I was mostly kidding about Ky," Star admitted. "He acts like a player, but I've hung out with him a few times and he's actually mega-cool. You could do way worse than him, you know?"

"I'll have to take that under advisement." Jade smiled. "The new Boysterous CD is totally sick—I play it all the time on my headphones."

Star nodded. "As for Eddie . . ." She hesitated, not wanting to say anything bad. "Well, you know his history with girls, right?"

Jade nodded. "Got it. It's okay. He's not really my type, anyway."

For the next few minutes they continued to gossip about a few of the other good-looking young stars in attendance. In the back of her mind, Star kept turning over what Jade had just revealed. *Mike would never, ever in a million years ask me to dump Missy for some new celebrity best friend just because it might help my career,* she thought, picturing her longtime best friend from back home. *Or to trade in Aaron for some flavor-of-the-month hunk, either.* She blushed slightly, as she usually did when thinking of her sort-of boyfriend, Aaron Bickford.

"Hey!" An angry voice interrupted the girls' conversation. "There you are."

Star glanced up to see Stan Starkey stomping over to them, glaring at Jade. Jade stared back at him sullenly. "I'm talking here, Stan," she snapped. "So shoot me, okay?"

"Look, I told you." Stan grabbed her by the arm. "This isn't a social occasion. You're supposed to be doing your job, not gossiping with your little friend here." He turned his glare toward Star.

Jade shook her arm free of his grasp. "Whatever," she said. "We were only talking for a minute."

"That's a minute too long. Now come on—I have some people you need to meet." Starkey strode away without bothering to glance back and see if Jade was following.

Jade hesitated for a second, then took a step after him. She paused just long enough to shoot Star an unreadable look. "See you, okay?" she muttered before hurrying after her manager.

Star stared after her as she disappeared into the crowd. "What was that all about?" she murmured under her breath. She'd already known that Jade's manager was kind of a jerk.

But could Jade be even unhappier than Star had realized? If so, what could she do to help?

Before she could figure out any answers, Mike and Tank hurried up to her. "There you are, sweetheart." Mike greeted her with a smile. "I think we've all put in enough time at this hoedown. Lola already headed upstairs, and Tank and I are fixin' to follow if you're ready to go."

Star nodded, suddenly realizing that she was exhausted. It had been a long day. "I'm ready," she said, stifling a yawn. "Let's blow this pop stand."

With one last backward glance in the direction Jade had disappeared, she followed Mike and Tank toward the door.

Five

"I don't know." Mike stared dubiously at the bit of fried egg on the end of his fork. "I don't much like the sound of this lunch or reception or whatever the heck it's s'posed to be. 'Specially not if Urbane's the one hostin' it."

"Eddie and Xandra are both hosting it," Star corrected him, stirring a little bit of milk into her tea. She and her team were sitting around the table in their hotel suite eating breakfast. "And Xandra's the one who invited me, not Eddie."

"But still . . ." Mike let his voice trail off as he popped the bite of egg into his mouth and chewed thoughtfully.

"Mike's right, babydoll," Lola put in, pushing up the sleeves of her vintage chenille bathrobe as she reached across the table for the sugar bowl. "You're better off staying as far away from that rotten Urbane kid as you possibly can." She blew on her coffee, which was giving off lazy coils of steam, and then dumped in several spoonfuls of sugar. "He's probably just trying to latch on to you again since your latest singles are number one and two on the charts this week."

Over the Top

"Numbers one and three, actually," Mags put in, pursing her lips.

Star hid her grin by bending down to slip Dudley a scrap of bacon under the table. Mags believed in being as accurate, precise, and careful as possible about everything. Lola . . . well, didn't. She often spoke before she thought and tended to have a sloppy approach to facts and figures that drove Mags bonkers. Considering how different they were, it was amazing that the two women got along as well as they did most of the time.

Lola shrugged and sipped her coffee. "Right, one and three, whatever," she said, seeming unperturbed by the correction. "My point is, our girl is hot stuff right now. Even more than usual, I mean. And Eddie's not doing quite so well—his latest is only, like, number fifteen or so, last I heard. Why wouldn't he try to grab on to Star's coattails again? It's not like he hasn't done it before."

Mike had set down his fork and was stroking his mustache as he gazed at Star. "Why in tarnation do you want to go to this lunch thing, anyway?" he asked her.

Star shrugged, fiddling with the piece of bacon on her plate. "I told you. It's because of what Xandra said. I know it's silly, and I'm sure Eddie has some kind of ulterior motive like you're saying, but I'm just curious. I want to hear what Xandra has to tell me about my aura or whatever. Not that I believe in that stuff," she added hurriedly. "It's just for fun, like Tank reading us our horoscopes every morning."

Tank looked up from the newspaper he was scanning and winked. "What do you mean? I believe every word of those horoscopes. Speaking of which, Star, your horoscope today says you should 'seek out new horizons and keep an open mind.'"

"Hear that, Mike?" Star exclaimed with a grin. "That means I *have* to go to this lunch thing. My horoscope is practically ordering me to do it!"

Mike snorted. "With reliable guidance like that, how can I say no?" he said sarcastically. Then he sighed. "Darlin', I just don't want you gettin' all excited and lettin' people take advantage of you."

"I hear you," Star said. The previous evening's conversation with Jade flashed through her mind. Once again she was grateful to have such a caring team behind her. How would she have survived the past two years in the spotlight without Mike and the others around to protect her and keep her happy? "And I know that Xandra's aura talk won't really help me find Mom and Dad and Timmy," she added. "But if I don't go, I'll go crazy wondering what she would've said. You know? Even if I know it doesn't really mean anything . . ." She spread out her hands hopelessly, not sure how to explain what she was feeling.

Mike sighed and shook his head. "Okay, okay," he said gruffly. He traded a long glance with Mags. "I suppose we'd better let you go, if it means that much to you."

"Thanks, Mike," Star said quietly, guessing that he was thinking back to what had happened the last time he'd put his foot down regarding the search for her family. That time, she had ended up alone on another continent thanks to Eddie's ulterior motives—and his private jet.

"Personally, I don't know why you'd want to spend any extra time with those people," Lola muttered, lifting her coffee cup to her lips.

Mike ignored Lola's comment. "But there's one condition," he told Star. "I want Tank to go over there first and check out the security setup at this restaurant. If he thinks it's too risky, the whole thing's off. Okay?"

"Deal," Star said, glancing over at her bodyguard.

Tank didn't meet her eye. In fact, he didn't even seem to be following the conversation anymore. He had lowered his newspaper and was staring blankly into space, a serene expression on his broad face.

"Tank?" Mike looked amused. "Looks like the engine's on but no one's drivin'," he commented to the others. "Yo, Tank!"

Tank snapped out of it, blinking several times and jerking his head around toward Mike. "What was that?" he said. "Sorry, I was just thinking about, er, something. . . ."

As Mike explained the plan again, Star gazed at Tank through slightly narrowed eyes. She had almost forgotten about his lovely young friend Anita.

I wonder if that's who he was thinking about just now? she thought with a smile. *I hope so—the two of them would be way cute together!*

"So, Tank," she said casually, reaching for another piece of toast, "did you have a good time at the reception last night?"

Tank shrugged his broad shoulders. "Little crowded for my taste, Star-baby," he said. "Good finger food, though. Did you get a chance to try those little fish-shaped hors d'oeuvres with the caviar on top?"

"No," Star said. "Um, did you and your friend Anita have some?"

Out of the corner of her eye she noticed Mike raise one eyebrow and glance over at Mags. But Star kept her gaze on Tank.

He met that gaze blandly. "Yep," he said. "They were tasty."
He glanced at his watch. "Want to head down to the gym in
a few minutes, short stuff? If we're going to get a workout in,
we'd better do it before this lunch party of yours."

"Sure," Star replied. "Just give me half an hour to digest my
breakfast and change clothes, okay?"

"Sounds like a plan." Folding his newspaper, Tank got up
and hurried off into another room.

Star leaned back in her chair, the remains of her breakfast
forgotten. If Tank had any romantic interest in Anita, he
didn't seem particularly eager to share it.

*I hope he's not going to pass up this chance just because he's
embarrassed or too devoted to his job or something,* she thought
worriedly. *It would be totally great for him to have a girlfriend;
he deserves one! Especially a nice one like Anita.*

A smile played across her lips. They would be in London
for two more days. Maybe she could figure out a way to
bring Tank and Anita together in a more-than-friends kind of
way . . . even if they never knew she was doing it.

It'll be a challenge, Star thought as she excused herself from
the table and hurried toward her bedroom with Dudley at
her heels. *But there's nothing I love more than a challenge!*

☆ ☆ ☆ ☆ ☆

"Whew," Star said, mopping her brow with a towel as she followed Tank toward the gym doors. They had just finished a brisk workout, and every muscle in Star's body felt pleasantly tired. "That was actually fun."

"Glad to hear it." Tank smiled down at her as he held open the door for her to exit. "We need to make sure we keep you in shape for dancing. You've got four shows to do next week, you know."

"I know." As Star stepped through the door, she saw Jade heading toward her. The other young singer was dressed in sweats with a towel slung over one arm. Stan's assistant, Manda, was right behind her, wearing a linen pantsuit and high heels and carrying a boom box.

"Hi!" Star called brightly. "You guys coming to work out? Tank and I just finished. The gym here is supernice!"

"Hello, Star," Manda cooed, her thin lips stretching into a sickly smile. "And Tank, it's so lovely to see you again." Her eyelashes fluttered wildly, as if a bug had just flown into one of her slightly bulging eyes.

"Ah, *mademoiselle*." Tank smiled politely. "Nice to see you, too."

Star hid a smile. Tank always called women *mademoiselle* when he couldn't remember their names. Usually they were so impressed with his flawless French accent that they never figured that out.

Sure enough, Manda looked overwhelmed at Tank's response. She put one bony hand to her heart and took a step closer. "Ooh, Mr. Massimo," she said, her lashes flapping harder than ever. "You're so charming!"

This time Star had to stop herself from rolling her eyes. If she wasn't mistaken, Manda was doing her best to flirt with Tank. Star couldn't really blame her—after all, Tank was a handsome and likable guy—but the neurotic, sour-tempered Manda wasn't quite the type of woman Star would choose for him.

"Come on, Manda," Jade grumbled, slapping her towel against her leg and looking bored. "I need to get this work-out over with if we're going to make it to that stupid luncheon on time."

"Luncheon?" Star repeated, suddenly distracted from her thoughts about Tank's love life. "You aren't talking about the lunch party thing Eddie Urbane and Xandra Om are throwing, are you?"

"Unfortunately, yeah." Jade rolled her eyes and moved closer to Star as Tank and Manda continued to chat with each other. "Stan's all up in my face about going, even though

I, like, barely know either of them. It's totally weak."

"I'm going too," Star told Jade.

"Shut up!" Jade exclaimed, sounding pleased. "Hey, at least I'll know one person there. Maybe we can hang out or something—if I can get away from Stan, I mean."

Star smiled, her mind kicking into gear. This could be just the chance she needed to figure out if Eddie was behind Xandra's sudden interest in Star's family. "Listen," she murmured, with a quick glance at the adults to make sure they weren't listening. She was just in time to see Manda run her long, pointy fuchsia fingernails up and down Tank's muscular arm. With a shudder Star returned her gaze to Jade. "Since we're both going to be there, do you think you could help me out with something . . . ?"

Six

"Star! Star! Over here! Smile, sweetheart!"

Star kept a pleasant expression on her face as she stepped across the sidewalk on Tank's arm. Although Xandra had described the gathering as a "lunch reception for a few selected guests," it seemed that every reporter in London had heard about it. There was an eager, shouting, shoving crowd of photographers taking up at least half a block outside the restaurant, with a dozen London police officers barely managing to keep a space open between the curb and the door.

Okay, this isn't quite what I was expecting, Star thought as her bodyguard hurried her through the restaurant's double glass doors. *But it will be worth it if I can figure out the truth about what Eddie and Xandra are up to.*

The party was packed. Dozens of guests sat at the small tables lining the walls, while countless more perched on stools along the bar and lined the stairs leading up to the small second-story balcony. Still more people milled around the open center of the room, including numerous reporters and cameramen. Star bit her lip, hoping that the crowd wasn't going to interfere with her plan. As she was looking around for Jade she heard someone calling her name.

"There you are, darling!" Xandra cried breathlessly as she swooped down on Star, throwing an arm around her shoulders. She was dressed in a long, flowing robelike dress that seemed to change color as she moved. Several large, gaudy crystals hung around her neck, and dozens of smaller ones were woven into her blond hair.

"Hi, Xandra," Star said, raising her voice over the noise of the party and trying not to wrinkle her nose at the woman's overwhelming peaches-and-patchouli scent. She was vaguely aware that several photographers were snapping their picture, while a few steps away Tank was keeping a careful eye on the crowd. "Thanks again for inviting me."

"We're so glad you could come." Xandra stepped back, grabbing Eddie out of the crowd nearby and yanking him forward to stand beside her. "Aren't we, darling?"

Eddie looked down at Star with disinterest. "Sure," he drawled. "It's a thrill." He glanced over at Tank. "Don't tell me y'all left the cowboy at home for once?" he added, slipping into an exaggerated parody of Mike's Texas accent. "Dangit, I'm sure he would've had a rootin' tootin' good time."

"I'm sure Mike's heartbroken to miss out on your usual perspicacity and badinage, Urbane," Tank replied pleasantly.

Eddie scowled, but Xandra ignored the exchange. She grabbed Star again, squeezing her hand. "Ooh, I can already tell it's going to be a good day to start uncovering your family's secrets. I can tell your aura is, you know, totally open and receptive; I'm already picking up all kinds of messages."

"Really?" Star said cautiously. "Like what?"

Xandra closed her eyes and took several deep breaths. "It's not easy to sort through them all," she intoned, waving her arms slowly through the air as if gathering stray psychic images to her bosom. "But I'm definitely getting a strong signal from a woman—I think it's your mother."

Star held her breath, not daring to speak. Even though she didn't really believe that Xandra was picking up messages from her aura, her heart started beating faster at the mention of her mother.

Xandra swayed slightly from side to side. "She's sending a message of love, unconditional love, and—"

"Eddie Urbane! There you are, hot stuff." Jade rushed up to the group at that moment, grabbing Eddie by the arm and planting a kiss on his cheek. Her dark eyes were sparkling, and she looked livelier and more beautiful than Star had ever seen her. "I've been looking everywhere for you."

Xandra's eyes flew open. Eddie grinned at Jade, his gaze slowly taking her in from head to toe. "Well, hello," he said, sounding surprised but gratified at the sudden attention. "You've met Xandra, right? Oh, and Star there."

Jade tossed her head, her long, glossy dark hair sliding over her shoulders. She barely glanced at Xandra, and didn't look at Star at all. "Yeah, hi," she said indifferently. Then she smiled beguilingly up at Eddie. "Listen, most of the peeps here are totally bootsie. Want to keep me company for a while so I don't die of boredom? I'd totally owe you."

Eddie looked pleased at Jade's attention. "Hey, I can't say no to a beautiful lady, right?" he said. "Be right back, Xan."

Xandra rolled her eyes as Jade pulled Eddie away. "Well, that was interesting," she muttered. Glancing at Star, she gave a short laugh. "Men, huh? Guess that's what I get for dating a teenager. . . . Anyway, where were we?"

Star held back a grin. Jade had played her part in their plan perfectly. Star had asked her to distract Eddie while she talked with Xandra. That way they would both get something they needed—Star would have a chance to find out if Xandra was sincere, while Jade could let her manager see her mingling with Eddie for a while.

Over the Top

"Can we find somewhere a little more private?" Star suggested, noticing several reporters edging closer.

"Oh, I really can't, darling," Xandra exclaimed. "I'm the cohost of the party—I have to stay in view!"

Star glanced up at the balcony at the far end of the room. While the steps leading up to it were crowded with party guests, the balcony itself was roped off and empty. "How about up there?" she suggested, gesturing toward it. "That way people can still see you, but we can talk without being overheard."

Xandra looked uncertain. "I really think I'd better stay down here."

"Oh, okay." Star shook her head, feigning regret. "Well, maybe we can do this another time . . ."

"No, no!" Xandra said quickly, putting a hand on Star's arm as if fearing she would leave the party that very moment. "I suppose it wouldn't hurt to duck up there for a few minutes. Come on."

Soon Star and Xandra were alone on the balcony overlooking the party. It was quieter up there, the noise of the crowd below more like a dull roar than a deafening racket. Tank had cleared the top few steps and was standing guard there.

"Now," Xandra said, taking Star by both hands and smiling

down at her. "Let's just see what we can feel. Open your senses, please. . . ."

She closed her eyes and took a series of deep breaths. Star waited, wondering what would happen next.

Eddie's nowhere in sight, she thought, quickly turning her head and scanning the crowd below while Xandra's eyes were closed. She noticed several photographers shooting their picture from various spots in the room, but there was no sign of Eddie or Jade anywhere. *He's not going to get any photo ops out of this if he doesn't turn up soon. So why is Xandra still going ahead with it? Is she just trying to gain my trust so Eddie can worm his way into my life again? Or does she maybe believe in this stuff after all?*

"Your mother wants you to know that she and the others are safe, Star," Xandra said in a low, dramatic voice.

Star took in a sharp breath, suddenly forgetting about Eddie. "Really?" she whispered. A vision of her parents and baby brother, smiling and happy, floated through her mind. "Where are they?"

Xandra hummed softly under her breath for a moment before answering. "The message is fading, going in and out," she murmured. "It's difficult to see exactly . . . but your mother is stretching her soul toward yours, trying to get her

74

message across. She says to never give up hope."

Star smiled. That sounded exactly like something her mother would say.

"She also says she's proud of you," Xandra continued. Her eyes were still closed, and her face looked pale and a little eerie in the dim light of the balcony. "They both are. Your father is sending something—it's a little harder to read him, but I think he's telling you to keep your spirit strong and your soul centered while you wait for their return."

Star's smile faded. *That doesn't sound like Dad at all*, she thought. *He always made fun of all that New Age mumbo jumbo.*

"Now your mother is back again," Xandra said. "She wants to keep trying to reach you, even if it doesn't all come through the first time. She says they're coming home soon. And when they do, she wants to do all the things she's missed doing with you—talking, hugging, shopping, gossiping, doing each other's hair, sharing a big, gooey chocolate sundae . . ."

This time Star shook her head. That definitely didn't sound like her mother—Ellie Calloway was allergic to chocolate. A few of the other activities on the list were questionable too. Star's mother didn't believe in gossip, and had little interest in playing with hair, whether her own or her daughter's.

Oh well, Star thought, holding back a sigh. *It's not like I*

really believed in this psychic connection thing anyway.

As Xandra continued swaying and muttering, Star leaned over and glanced downstairs again. The crowd was bigger and noisier than ever, but she still couldn't see Eddie or Jade anywhere.

That's odd, she told herself, returning to her earlier thoughts. *Xandra and I have been up here for a while now, and I'm sure every photographer in the room has gotten at least a few pictures of us together. If this is a big publicity stunt for Eddie, wouldn't he make sure to stick around and be a part of it? I mean, I know he has sort of a short attention span, but really . . .*

"Star? Are you okay, darling?"

Star realized that Xandra had opened her eyes and was staring at her. She forced a smile. "Sorry," she said. "I guess I was just, um, overwhelmed by what you're saying."

"I understand." Xandra gave Star's hands an extra squeeze. "We can stop if you—oh! Your mother is sending another message, a song this time . . ." She started humming, then singing the opening lyrics to "Star Bright."

Star gulped. *She's good,* she thought. *I wonder how she knew that song is so important to me?*

For a second she was tempted to reconsider her skepticism. Then she thought about it a little more, realizing that anyone who'd ever glanced at her Web site, read an article about her, or seen her biography show on PopTV knew that she'd been named after that song. It wasn't a mystical connection to her mother—there was no such thing. Whether she really believed what she was saying or was totally faking it, Xandra had no more idea where Star's family might be than anyone else.

Star gulped, surprised at how depressing it was to accept that. "Sorry, Xandra," she said, interrupting the woman's slightly off-key crooning. "I—I'm feeling sort of tired. I think I'd better go."

Politely brushing off Xandra's entreaties to stay a little longer, she looked around once more for Jade, hoping to let the other girl know she was leaving. But there was still no sign of her.

Oh well, she thought. *I guess she'll figure it out. Either that, or she already got sick of listening to Eddie brag about himself and she took off.*

She hurried to the steps, where Tank was waiting. "Ready to go, Star-baby?"

Star nodded and sighed. "Let's get out of here."

☆ ☆ ☆ ☆ ☆

"Just a sec," Lola said, leaning across the limo to dab a little extra gloss onto Star's lips. She leaned back and smiled proudly at her handiwork. "There! Now you're ready to face the cameras, babydoll."

"Thanks, Lola," Star said, brushing a piece of lint off the skirt of her long, sleek lavender dress. She glanced over at Mike, who was sitting beside her. "Ready?"

Mike peered out the limo window. "Looks like quite a crowd out there," he commented. "Just do your thing, smile and answer a few questions if you want, and we'll have you inside as quick as a hiccup."

Star nodded. A moment later Tank swung open her door and offered a hand to help her out of the car. A roar went up from the crowd as she straightened up and stepped forward.

As usual it took a few seconds for her eyes to adjust to the lights and flashbulbs. She smiled and waved, allowing Tank and Mike to guide her across the sidewalk and onto the red carpet leading into the auditorium. Reporters and photographers crowded against the metal barricades on either side, shouting and jostling for a better position.

Star took a few steps away from the men and struck a pose, one foot angled slightly in front of the other as Lola had taught her, smiling and waving to the paparazzi. For one dizzying second, she was sure she must have showed up at the Notey Awards or some movie premiere by mistake. *This couldn't possibly be a memorial program for someone who just died, could it?* she wondered as multiple voices howled her name and eagerly called out questions. *Too weird . . .*

"Star! Star!" a nearby reporter shrieked, waving her hand frantically. "How well did you know Ernie Golden?"

Star paused in front of the reporter. "Not that well, unfortunately," she said. "I only met him a few times. But my manager knew him for many years and thought the world of him."

Other reporters shouted out more questions, most of them having to do with Ernie Golden or that evening's event. Star answered them patiently as she continued to smile and pose for pictures.

Finally Mike stepped forward. "Time to move along," he murmured in Star's ear.

She nodded. "I have to get inside," she told the crowd. "Is there one more question? Yes?" She pointed to a young reporter nearby.

"Star!" he cried. "Would you care to comment on your very close friendship with Eddie Urbane and Xandra Om?"

Star blinked in surprise. "Er, they're both very nice people, very talented," she said. "Thanks for your support! You guys are great!" With a last quick wave, she allowed Mike and Tank to hustle her inside, with Mags and Lola following behind.

Soon they were inside. The auditorium was buzzing with activity as hundreds of people milled around, all of them dressed in their finest designer evening wear. The stage was hidden behind a velvet curtain, and soft music played over the sound system. An usher showed Star and her team to their seats. Star had a spot in the front row, over to the left side of the stage. Mike was seated beside her, and the others were assigned spots directly behind them.

"That was a weird question," Star commented to Mike as they sat down on the plush velvet seats. "The one about Eddie and Xandra, I mean."

Mike shrugged, tugging at his sleeve. "Some newspaper probably published a photo of you three from the reception last night," he said. "Don't fret about it."

"Don't worry, I won't." Star glanced at the empty seat beside her. "Hey, did you get a chance to request that Jade sit by me?"

"Called the seating people this mornin'." Mike stretched his long legs into the open space in front of their seats, which allowed most of his purple cowboy boots to show beneath the hems of his tuxedo pants. "Never heard back, though, so I'm not sure what's happenin' with that."

"That's okay, I— Oh! There she is now!" Star suddenly spotted Jade coming up the aisle with Starkey and Manda right behind her. She waved vigorously. "Jade! Over here!"

Jade saw her and waved back. She hurried over. "Yo, Star," she said, yanking impatiently at the long purple scarf she was wearing over her slinky black dress. She gave Star a small but real smile. "What's up?"

"Are you sitting with us?" Star asked eagerly. "There's an empty seat right here."

"I think I—"

"Jade!" Starkey's gravelly voice cut her off. He stomped up to his client, completely ignoring Star and Mike. "Quit blabbing, and let's go find our seats. I insisted that they seat us in the middle, not out here in no-man's-land."

Jade scowled at him. "Chill out, Stan," she said. "I'm just trying to talk to people here, okay? Isn't that what you're always up in my grille about doing? Anyway, I think I'd rather hang here with Star than sit with whatever boring old fart you picked out."

"Too bad," Stan snapped. "We're out of here."

Jade crossed her arms over her chest, almost yanking off

her purple scarf in the process. "No way," she said.

Stan's face darkened. "Look here, little girl . . . ," he began hotly.

Mike stood up, looking alarmed. "Listen, Stan," he said. "I think we need to cool down and—"

Suddenly a cheery voice interrupted the tense moment. "Hello, hello!" Xandra cried, rushing up to them with Eddie in tow. "It's so fabulous to see you all here tonight! Everyone looks so wonderful!"

For once Star was relieved to see Eddie and his girlfriend. "Hi, guys," she said. "Where are you sitting?"

Xandra smiled at her. "Oh, did you want us to sit here with you, Star?" she exclaimed. "How sweet! Don't mind if we do, right, Eddie?"

Star tilted her head in surprise as Xandra pushed past Jade and Starkey and flopped into the seat beside Star. Seeming completely oblivious to the tense scene she'd just interrupted, Xandra crossed her long legs and started arranging the complicated ribbonlike skirt of her red gown.

Eddie slouched forward and flopped into the seat on Xandra's other side. "How's it going, everyone?" he muttered to the group at large.

"Ah, Urbane." Starkey gave what he probably thought was

a friendly smile, though Star thought it looked more like a shark gnashing its teeth. "Nice to see you again, young man." He nudged at Jade, who was staring at the newcomers in astonishment. "Mind if we join you?"

"Guess not," Eddie said with a disinterested shrug, picking at his fingernails.

With a quick glance at Star, Jade sank into the seat beside Eddie, while Starkey took the spot on her other side. At that moment an usher appeared and glanced down the row, looking slightly alarmed.

"Excuse me," he said. "Our seating chart . . ."

"Could I speak to you for a moment about that, sir?" Mike said immediately, putting an arm around the usher's shoulder and steering him away into the aisle.

Xandra put one manicured hand to her face and giggled. "Oopsie!" she trilled. "I hope we didn't cause any trouble by sitting here. I think we were supposed to be over on the other side of the auditorium."

"I'm sure Mike will take care of it," Star said. She wasn't thrilled to be sitting next to Xandra instead of Jade. But at least the ugly scene between Jade and her manager seemed to be over.

Too bad poor Jade got stuck next to Eddie, though, Star thought, halfway between sympathetic and amused. *Especially after spending so much time with him earlier today! I'll have to try to make it up to her somehow.*

Just then Mike returned. He took his seat again, straightening his bow tie.

"Everything okay?" Star asked him as Xandra turned away to speak to Eddie.

"Hunky-dory." Mike smiled and winked at her. He glanced down the row and lowered his voice. "I convinced that fella to adjust his chart. Thought that might be the best way to avoid trouble."

Lola leaned forward from her seat behind them and poked Star in the shoulder. "Lucky Urbane didn't end up next to you," she whispered. "That way he can't claim you're his date tonight."

Star giggled. "Don't worry, Lola," she whispered back. "I don't think Xandra would allow that."

"Hmm?" Xandra turned toward Star with a bright smile. "Did I hear my name?"

Star smiled back weakly. "Er, yes," she said. "Um, Lola was just asking who designed your dress."

Xandra started chattering eagerly in response to her query. For the next few minutes Star nodded and pretended to be interested as Xandra moved from talking about her gown to various other topics, hardly pausing for a breath. Farther down the row she noticed that Jade and Eddie were also talking to each other, though judging by the gloomy expressions on their faces, neither of them was having much fun. Star felt a stab of sympathy for Jade.

That feeling only increased when, during a momentary lull in Xandra's monologue about something or other, she caught a bit of Starkey's loud conversation with the man seated on his far side. "I can't believe they didn't get their act together and put Jade on the bill tonight," he was saying with great irritation. "She really should be up there onstage—it would be a much better show, if you ask me."

"Nobody asked you, Stan," Jade muttered, looking embarrassed.

Star winced. Why did Starkey have to embarrass his client in front of a bunch of people who were little more than strangers? She just didn't understand how he could be so unpleasant all the time.

"Anyway, Star," Xandra said, breaking into Star's thoughts, "I was thinking about our session earlier today."

"Session?" Star repeated blankly, for a moment imagining herself and Xandra in a recording studio with musicians.

"Our spiritual session," Xandra said. "When I contacted your parents earlier today, remember?"

"Oh, right. That." Star was tempted to let Xandra know exactly what she'd thought of that "session," but she held her tongue. If Xandra was just buddying up to her on Eddie's behalf, that was one thing. But if, by chance, she actually believed in her own psychic talents, Star didn't want to hurt her feelings.

Xandra put a hand on her arm. "I really feel like we're connecting on this, Star," she said. "I'm sure we could make a real breakthrough with a little more time. Maybe I should come on tour with you for a while—you know, travel with you, be your spiritual guide and see if we can reach the truth and find your family."

"What a nice offer," Star said, doing her best to hide her alarm at the idea of Xandra joining the tour. Whether Xandra really had any sort of psychic connection with anything at all, her over-the-top personality was already becoming tiresome. "Um, I'll think about it, okay?"

Just then the lights flashed several times. Spotlights swirled around on the velvet curtain in front of them, which slowly rose to reveal a huge black-and-white photo of Ernie Golden hanging over the stage. Star stared up at it, suddenly remembering why they were all there that night.

As the live band hidden away in the orchestra pit struck up a medley of hits Golden had produced, Star settled back in her seat. Putting Xandra, Jade, and everything else out of her mind, she prepared to enjoy the show.

Seven

"Thank you, everyone. Thank you all so very much."

Up on the stage, which was illuminated with a series of soft blue and gold spotlights, Athena Quincy bowed to the audience. She was wearing a long black gown set with jewels that gleamed delicately in the stage lights.

In the front row Star clapped wildly. She had enjoyed every moment of the memorial show so far, from an opening retrospective of Golden's career narrated by Charles Maestro, the famous Hollywood actor, to performances by a dozen famous singers and musicians, all of whom had worked with Golden at one time or another.

Then Athena had come onstage. After sharing a few of her personal memories of Golden, she had begun to sing. It was the first time Star had ever seen Athena perform live, and she was impressed with the way the diva commanded the stage and the audience. There was no way anyone could look away. Even Xandra, who had wriggled and whispered throughout much of the show, fell silent as the first notes poured out of the diva's throat.

As the applause began to die down, Athena shifted the microphone to her other hand. "Thank you," she said again. "Next I'd like to perform a little number that was always one of Ernie's favorites. Maybe some of you will remember it—it's called 'Star Bright.'"

Star gasped. She had hoped that Athena might perform that song, though she hadn't really expected it. "Star Bright" had been a hit for the singer, but not one of her biggest, and Star had guessed that it might not make the bill.

She felt someone poke her in the back. "Too cool!" Lola whispered in her ear.

Star just nodded, not daring to take her eyes off Athena as the band played the familiar opening notes of the song. She found herself mouthing the lyrics along with Athena, at least until the singer departed from the recorded version to add a few dramatic runs and a touching ad lib referring to Golden by name. By the end of the song Star was so overwhelmed that her eyes filled with tears, though she struggled not to let any escape, not wanting to mess up her makeup.

"Yay!" she yelled, leaping to her feet without realizing it and applauding loudly. Beside her Mike rose as well, and soon the rest of their row joined her. Before long the entire audience was on its feet.

"Wow!" Xandra said brightly as she clapped. "She's good, isn't she?"

Noticing a photographer crouching in front of the stage taking pictures of their row, Star refrained from rolling her eyes. "Yeah," she said. "She's good."

The show ended a few minutes later. As the lights came up Mike leaned toward Star. "The after party for this shindig is back at our hotel," he murmured. "Feel like stopping in for a few?"

"Sure," Star said.

Xandra leaned over from her other side. "Did you say you guys are going to the after party?" she asked. "That's fabulous! Eddie and I were planning to go too. Shall we ride over together?"

Star gulped. But before she could answer, Mike shook his head. "Sorry, Miz Om," he said. "Sounds lovely, but I'm afraid our limo is full up as it is. We'll just have to see y'all over there."

"Oh." Xandra sounded disappointed. Then she shrugged.

"Oh well," she said. "At least we can all walk out together, right?"

Star leaned forward to see if Jade had enjoyed the show. But before she could call out to her, a cluster of photographers appeared in front of their seats and started snapping pictures.

"Come on," Mike said, standing up and offering Star his hand. "We'd better hightail it outta here before we get stuck."

"Good idea." Star smoothed her skirt and stood up.

Lola hurried around from her seat, compact in hand. "Hold still, sugar," she murmured as Tank and Mike moved to block Star from view with their bodies.

Star closed her eyes and waited while Lola quickly touched up her face and fluffed her hair. Nearby she could hear Eddie whining about the crowd.

"Oh, hush up," Xandra told him, sounding a little impatient. "It won't kill you to pose for a few more photos on our way out. Just means a better chance of making the papers tomorrow, right?"

"Ready," Lola said to Star at that moment, stepping back.

Star opened her eyes and glanced around. Xandra and Eddie were still standing nearby watching the nearest photographer shoot pictures of another celebrity a little farther down the row. Jade and her manager had disappeared, though Star soon spotted them a short distance away talking with some people she didn't recognize.

"Let's hit the trail," Mike said, gesturing for Mags to join them. "It's not gettin' any earlier."

"Oh, are you guys leaving now?" Xandra called as Mike led the way out toward the main aisle. "Hold up; we'll come with you."

It took a while to make their way out of the auditorium. There were many more celebrities and VIPs in attendance that night than had come to the party the evening before, and most of them wanted to stop Mike or Star to say hello. But eventually Star and her team found themselves standing in front of the exit door. Xandra and Eddie, who were still trailing along after them, had paused to talk to a reporter a few yards back.

"I'm sure there'll be more paparazzi outside," Mike told Star. "This time let's just smile and wave and keep moving, okay?"

Star nodded. She prepared herself as Tank opened the door and led the way outside. Sure enough, dozens of photographers were lining the walkway, their cameras at the ready.

"Star! Star! What did you think of the program?" someone shouted.

"Star! Smile this way, sweetheart! Star!"

"Hey Star! Over here; what did you think of Athena's performance?"

Although Star was trying to follow Mike's advice to keep moving, she couldn't resist the last question. She paused and turned on her heel, searching the crowd for the reporter who had asked it. "Athena was spectacular," she said as cameras flashed all around her. "She's a truly amazing performer, and I was honored to be here to watch her tonight. Thank you."

She started to move on, but suddenly she felt someone fling an arm around her. Glancing up, expecting to find that it was Tank or Lola, she instead saw Xandra smiling out at the reporters. "That's right!" Xandra cried. "Eddie and I—get over here, Eddie." She reached over and grabbed Eddie's sleeve, dragging him to stand on her other side. "As I was saying, Eddie and I just adored Athena's performance. I'm sure it made Ernie Golden's spirit dance."

Cameras flashed again. After a moment Tank stepped forward, pulling Star away. "All right," he said in his gruffest scary-bodyguard voice. "That's enough. We have to be going."

He hustled Star out toward the limo awaiting them at the curb. Soon she and the rest of the team were safely inside.

"Well, that was interestin'," Mike said darkly as Tank took the wheel from the valet and steered them out toward the street.

Star glanced at him. "What, you mean Xandra and Eddie?" She shrugged and giggled. "At least Eddie finally found a girlfriend who's as big a camera hog as he is."

Mags pursed her lips. "Indeed," she said succinctly, folding her hands on the lap of her tailored navy blue dress.

Star started to say more but was suddenly overwhelmed by a big yawn. "Whew!" she said, grabbing hold of the door handle as the car swerved around a pothole. "Guess I'm more tired than I thought."

Mike looked at her with concern. "Sure you're up to the after party?" he asked. "We don't have to go at all."

"No, I'm okay," Star insisted. "Besides, I want to see if I can talk to Jade for a minute. And maybe talk to Athena again too."

"All right," Mike said, straightening his jacket. "Reckon we can stop in for a little while then, as planned, and then head upstairs to hit the hay."

The party, which was taking place in an even bigger and fancier ballroom than the one from the evening before, was already crowded when they arrived. After making her way past the usual phalanx of photographers near the door, Star glanced around the room. Mike stepped away to speak with an acquaintance, while Mags and Lola made their way toward the bar, leaving Star with Tank.

"Wow," she said, coughing slightly as a tendril of stray cigarette smoke drifted past. "There are a lot of people here."

Tank nodded. "Stick close to me tonight, okay, short stuff?" he said. "It's probably not safe for you to go wandering off, or . . ."

His voice drifted off, and Star glanced up at him curiously. He was staring out across the room. When she followed his gaze, she immediately spotted Anita standing in the crowd, holding a glass of wine and talking to a small group of people who looked like musicians.

"Hey!" Star blurted out. "There's your friend Anita."

With everything else that had been going on that day, she'd once again almost forgotten about Tank's potential girlfriend. Now she was happier than ever that they had decided to attend the party.

"Listen, Tank," she said quickly, spotting Eddie and Xandra entering the room with several bodyguards trailing behind them. "I—um, I wanted to talk to Xandra a little more about the whole psychic thing. Why don't you go hang out with

Anita or something? Eddie's bodyguards can keep an eye on me for a while."

"Huh?" Tank blinked down at her, then glanced toward Eddie and his group. "Oh. Are you sure?"

"Definitely," Star assured him. "I'll be fine, I swear."

Before Tank could respond, she turned and hurried over toward the others. Glancing over her shoulder, she saw Tank watching her go, looking worried. A second later Anita appeared at his side. With one last glance after Star, Tank turned to talk with the woman.

Star nodded with satisfaction. Maybe now she could get somewhere with her plan to get Tank together with Anita.

Then she realized what she'd done. Eddie had already disappeared into the crowd, but Xandra seemed thrilled to see her. She immediately pushed past Eddie's bodyguards and grabbed Star by the arm. "There you are, sweetie," she said enthusiastically. "I was hoping you'd be here so we could chat some more."

Star forced a smile. "Here I am!"

She did her best to appear interested as Xandra launched into a long, rambling monologue about her own psychic powers, and various related topics.

Okay, so maybe this isn't exactly how I wanted to spend the rest

of my evening, she thought, holding in a sigh as she scanned the constantly shifting crowd for Athena or Jade. She eventually glimpsed Athena halfway across the room, almost completely surrounded by well-wishers and photographers. Jade was nowhere in sight, nor were Tank and Anita. *I just hope Tank appreciates it. . . .*

For the next twenty minutes she kept an eye out for her bodyguard or his friend. She didn't see them, though Mags did wander past at one point and shoot Star, Xandra, and Eddie's bodyguards a curious look. Star was tempted to call her over, but before she could, the crowd shifted again and Mags disappeared from sight. Star swallowed a sigh and tried to look interested as Xandra rambled on.

After a few more minutes she realized that Xandra was, once again, talking about joining her on tour so she could read Star's aura full-time. Star tuned back in to the conversation, realizing that the occasional "mm-hmms" she was contributing might be encouraging Xandra.

". . . and even if we can't work out all the details before you leave London, I'm sure I could fly over to meet you in Ireland for a couple of days," Xandra babbled eagerly. "Maybe I could hang out backstage while you perform some of your concerts—that's probably when your spiritual energy is the highest, so it might give me more to work with."

"Oh, I don't know," Star said, suddenly wishing that Mike or Mags was around to intervene for her. She was starting to doubt that Xandra's true motives had anything to do with finding Star's family, or even gaining more publicity for Eddie. Why hadn't she figured it out sooner? "I think I'm supposed to be pretty busy in Ireland. You know— interviews and stuff. It would be way boring for you to hang around through all of that."

"That's all right," Xandra said cheerfully. "How about France, then? That's your next stop, right? And I just adore Paris, so that would work out great! We could stroll along the Seine; the spiritual energy is fabulous there. Or else I could join you when you start the Asian leg of the tour—I've always wanted to visit Japan anyway. . . ."

Star grimaced, again not sure what to say. She was trying to come up with a polite but firm response when there was a sudden commotion nearby. Glancing over, she saw a pair of Eddie's bodyguards restraining Stan Starkey.

"Let me through, you steroidal goons!" Starkey blustered, his face red and his thin black hair flopping forward over his face as he struggled against the guards. "Don't you know who I am?"

"It's okay, guys," Xandra called out. "You can let him through."

Starkey shot the guards a dirty look as they released him. Straightening his dark suit and running a hand over his head to smooth back his hair, he stepped toward Star and Xandra.

"You," he snarled at Star. "What have you done with Jade?"

Star blinked at him in surprise. "Huh?" she said, startled by the fury in his eyes. "What do you mean? I haven't seen Jade since we left the auditorium."

Starkey glowered at her. "Don't lie to me, little girl," he snapped. "Jade told Manda that she was going to hang out with you here at the party since you two didn't get to sit together at the concert." He rolled his eyes. "Immature brat," he muttered under his breath.

"She—she said that?" Star said weakly, hardly daring to contradict him when he looked so angry. "Um, maybe she's still looking for me or something, I don't—"

"Star!" Jade exclaimed breathlessly, rushing up to the group at that moment, her purple scarf flying out behind her. Eddie's bodyguards made a halfhearted move to stop her, but she shoved past them without pausing. "There you are, girl. I told you I'd be right back from the bathroom—did you get us those sodas we were talking about?"

Star gulped, belatedly catching on. Before she could say anything, Starkey glared at Jade. "The jig is up, you little liar," he growled at Jade. "What's the big idea, sneaking off like that? Talk about stupid—anything could've happened to you!"

Star winced. Starkey was mostly expressing the same concerns that Mike or Tank might in a similar situation. But he was expressing them in a way Mike and Tank never would. Once again she felt a flash of deep pity for the other girl. Even all the fame and money and number-one records in the world couldn't possibly make up for living with Starkey's sour attitude all the time.

"I told Manda where I was going," Jade said, sounding desperate. She sneaked an anxious glance at Star. "Star and I—"

"Star and you nothing," Starkey interrupted. He jerked a thumb in Star's direction. "She already told me she hadn't seen you since the show. You're busted."

Star's heart sank as Jade shot her an indecipherable look. *I can't believe I gave her away*, she thought miserably. *She needed me to cover for her—probably so she could get a few minutes' peace without Starkey and Manda harping on her—and I blew it. And after she just helped me out so much earlier today by distracting Eddie . . .*

Over the Top

"Listen," she blurted out, trying to fix things in any way she could. "Um, I didn't understand what you were asking before, Mr. Starkey. See, I thought you were asking where Jade was right this minute, um, and I didn't know which bathroom she'd gone to, or . . ."

But Star was a terrible liar, and she soon let her voice trail off; she wasn't even convincing herself. Starkey ignored her completely as he grabbed Jade by the wrist.

"Come on," he said through gritted teeth, a vein bulging out on his neck. "Let's go." Star could do nothing but watch as he dragged Jade away.

"Well, shoot," a familiar voice murmured from just behind Star. "That was kinda ugly."

Star glanced up over her shoulder at Mike. "It's all my fault," she said, tears springing to her eyes.

Mike let out a deep sigh. Pushing past Xandra, who was already babbling excitedly to one of the guards about what had just happened, he led Star to a relatively quiet corner of the room. Then he stood facing her.

"Look, sweetheart," he said, his voice gentle. "I didn't hear everything back there, but I got the gist. And there ain't no way you should go blamin' yourself for any of it."

"But if I'd realized . . . ," Star began.

Mike cut her off by shaking his head. "Look, I've known Stan Starkey since round about the Stone Age," he said. "And plenty more of his type besides. This business seems to attract 'em like a swamp attracts skeeters, unfortunately. People who are meaner'n a skillet full of rattlesnakes, and don't mind takin' it out on other people when things don't go their way."

Despite her distress, Star couldn't help smiling slightly at Mike's colorful expressions. "But not everyone in the music business is like that," she said. "You're not."

"Sure hope not." Mike smiled at her. "And you're right— there's a whole mess of good people in this biz as well. People like Ernie Golden, f'rinstance. Nobody ever had a bad word to say about him, because he cared about people and music more than anything—and in that order."

Star nodded slowly. She understood what Mike was saying, but that didn't make her feel much better about what had just happened. "But Jade . . ."

"Jade is a smart young lady, and a talented one," Mike said. "She'll figure out before long that Starkey's just holdin' her back, or I miss my guess. In the meantime, though, you can't do much more to help her than keep on bein' her friend as much as she'll let you. Okay?"

Star bit her lip. She didn't want to accept what Mike was saying, though she knew he was probably right. He usually was.

"Okay," she said at last. "I guess."

"That's my girl." Mike smiled and reached down for a hug. "Now come on. Let's round up the others and head upstairs. I don't know about you, but I'm beat."

Star nodded, her mind racing with everything that had happened that day—Xandra and Eddie's behavior, Athena's performance, the scene just now with Starkey, and more. She was tired, too. But she suspected it would be a long time before she fell asleep that night.

Eight

"Who'd be callin' us so early?" Mike muttered, glancing at his watch as the phone rang in the suite the next morning. Star was sitting at the table having breakfast with her manager, Mags, and Lola. Tank had just departed to take Dudley for his morning walk.

"I'll get it." Mags set down her coffee cup and hurried toward the phone.

Star yawned and poked at her oatmeal. "Maybe it's Tricia or one of the other publicists. They never seem to notice what time it is."

Mike shook his head as Mags picked up the receiver. "Doubt it," he said. "They generally call me on my cell, not the room phone."

Mags put her hand over the mouthpiece and glanced over at them, her expression slightly disapproving. "It's Ms. Om, calling for Star," she told Mike. "What shall I tell her?"

"Tell her it's rude to call so dang early," Lola put in. "We all had a pretty late night last night. How did she know we weren't still sleeping?"

Star grinned. "She just knew," she said in a spooky, quavery voice, wriggling her fingers in the air. "She's a little bit psychic, remember?"

Lola rolled her eyes. "More like a little bit psycho," she muttered.

Mike glanced over at Mags. "Just get rid of her."

"No, wait," Star said, feeling slightly guilty for making fun of Xandra behind her back. Besides, there was something she needed to say to her. "I'll talk to her. No big deal." She got up and took the phone from Mags. "Hello?"

"Star! Good morning!" Xandra's breathless voice greeted her. "It's a fabulous day, isn't it?"

Glancing out the window at the overcast London sky, Star shrugged. "I guess."

"Oh, it is," Xandra assured her. "I can practically feel the spiritual energy zinging around in the ether. Should we meet in the park or something and take advantage? I have a feeling we could make some real breakthroughs today."

Star grimaced. Even without her suspicions, the last thing she would have felt like doing was spending more time with

Xandra. "I don't think I can," she said. "I have some stuff to do this morning, and a business lunch to go to after that. And then the funeral is this afternoon, so . . ."

"Oh, but this is so important!" Xandra said urgently. "I'm sure you could change your schedule, couldn't you?"

"Sorry, I don't think so." Star tried to make her voice a little firmer. Xandra had to be one of the pushiest people she'd ever met. How was she ever going to get rid of her? If she just came out and told her what she suspected about her motives, Star was sure Xandra would only deny it and insist on having a spiritual conference about it or something.

Mike stood up and wandered closer. "Want me to speak to her, Star?" he murmured. "I'll make sure she knows that no means no."

Star waved him away, suddenly struck with an idea. "Um, I'm really pretty busy all morning," she told Xandra. "But come to think of it, maybe I could meet up with you for a few minutes before the funeral this afternoon. How about that?"

"Sure," Xandra responded immediately. "How about two o'clock at the little Indian place around the corner? You know, the one everyone's raving about. I've been dying to try it, but Eddie hates Indian food. I could grab a table up front and watch for you."

Over the Top

"I think that might take too long," Star said, wincing at the thought of sitting in a restaurant window with Xandra for the world to see. "Why don't we just meet here at the hotel? How about that little lounge outside the main ballroom?"

"Oh," Xandra said. "But that's . . . Well, if you think going out would take too long, we could just meet in the hotel lobby. That would be easier than the lounge. How does that sound?"

"I think the lounge is a better spot," Star said firmly. "I'll be there at two thirty. Okay? Then maybe we can head over to the funeral together or something."

"Well, okay." Xandra sounded a little happier at that idea. "See you then."

As Star hung up the phone Mike scowled at her. "What in blue blazes was that all about?" he exclaimed, sounding irritated. "Why'd you let her bully you like that, Star?"

"Don't burst a blood vessel," Star told him with a smile. "I didn't let her bully me. I have a plan."

Mike raised an eyebrow, looking surprised but slightly mollified. "A plan?"

"What kind of plan? Spill it, babydoll," Lola urged.

Star sat down at the table and glanced around at the three

adults. "See, I think I've finally figured out what Xandra's up to," she explained. "And I'm afraid she'll just keep pestering me if I don't give her a reason not to. Because of the free publicity."

"You mean you think Urbane's putting her up to this?" Lola asked, a frown darkening her face as it usually did when Eddie's name came up.

Star shook her head. "Nope, I don't think we can blame Eddie this time," she said. "I assumed he was behind it at first too. But Xandra's just as happy to hang out around me whether he's there or not—as long as there are cameras nearby. I think *she's* the one who's after publicity."

"Hmm." Mike raised his coffee cup to his lips and gazed at her over the rim. He took a sip and then lowered the cup. "Very perceptive, darlin'."

Star gazed at him, noting his lack of surprise and realizing that he'd probably figured out what was going on ages ago. She sighed, thinking back over her contact with Xandra over the past two days and wishing she'd been a little quicker on the uptake. "At first I thought she was just being nice," she said. "But why would someone in her twenties be so eager to hang out with a fourteen-year-old like me?"

"Hey, I like to hang out with you, and *I'm* in my twenties,"

Lola put in with a wink. "My late twenties, that is."

Star grinned at her. Lola was in her forties, though she didn't dress or act like it. "I know, I know," she said. "But it's not just that; it's the whole way she acted around me. She was always trying to get the two of us in front of the cameras together, you know?"

"Okay, makes sense, I guess. But are you sure Eddie isn't involved in this somehow?" Lola asked.

"Maybe, but I doubt it." Star shrugged. "In fact, I wonder if Xandra only started dating Eddie in the first place because being with him puts her in the spotlight, maybe helps jump-start her acting career or whatever. You know? I mean, why else would she date a seventeen-year-old, no matter how cute he is?"

Lola still looked uncertain, but Mags nodded and Mike smiled at Star. "Very smart, sweetheart," he said, reaching across the table to give her a pat on the shoulder. "I've been suspectin' Ms. Om for some time now, but I wanted to let you figure it out for yourself if possible. I'm proud of you."

Star grinned at him. "See? I can totally learn from the past."

"But if you know all this, why did you agree to meet with her this afternoon?" Mags put in, sounding worried.

"You aren't plannin' to confront her or some such, are

you?" Mike asked, stroking his mustache. "Because I don't think that's such a hot idea. I've run into Xandra's type before, and they can be pretty ruthless and conniving, 'specially when they feel cornered."

Star just smiled. "That's all part of my plan," she said, glancing over at Mags and Lola. "I just need a little help. . . ."

At two thirty on the dot, Star stopped just before a corner at the end of the hotel hallway and glanced over at Tank. "Okay," she said. "Ready to do this?"

Tank nodded. "Ready when you are," he said. "I'm just going to hang back and play dumb—this plan is all you. But if you feel uncomfortable, just give me a signal and we're out of there."

"Thanks." Star took a deep breath as the two of them rounded the corner and headed on toward the meeting spot. The hallway was deserted and silent. Tank reached the lounge door and pushed it open, standing back for Star to step through.

"Star! You made it!" Xandra leaped up from her seat on one of the low, plush sofas that lined the elegantly decorated room.

Star wasn't the least bit surprised to see a stylishly dressed young man wearing sunglasses sitting on another sofa. He stood when Star entered.

"Hi, Xandra," Star said. "I'm sure you remember my body-guard, Tank Massimo." She gestured toward Tank, who nodded politely. Then Star glanced pointedly toward the strange man.

"Yes, of course," Xandra said, shooting Tank a brief smile. Then she glanced back at the other man. "Oh, and I hope you don't mind—this is my biographer, George. He's very interested in watching me at work; I didn't think you'd mind if he observed."

"Your biographer?" Star said politely. "How interesting." She avoided looking at Tank, afraid that she would start to laugh if she caught his eye. She was pretty sure she recognized the young "biographer" as one of the newer reporters for PopTV News.

Xandra took Star by the arm. "Come, let's sit down and do some breathing and centering exercises together, shall we?"

"Okay," Star said. "But first I need to use the ladies' room. Please excuse me for a second."

She hurried into the restroom at the far end of the lounge. Once inside she leaned against one of the sinks, staring at herself in the mirror. Would her plan work? Or would she turn out to be all wrong about Xandra's motives? She felt a twinge of doubt but shook it off.

"Time to find out the truth," she muttered. "*Carpe diem* and all that . . ."

Stepping away from the sinks, she glanced briefly down the row of toilet stalls. Then she cracked open the door leading out to the lounge.

"Xandra?" she called. "Could you come in here a second? I need help with my zipper—it's stuck."

"Coming, Star!" Xandra called back immediately. A moment later she joined Star in the bathroom. "What's the problem, darling?" she asked breathlessly. "Let's get it fixed and get back out there. We don't have much time before—"

"Hold it, Xandra," Star interrupted briskly. "I didn't really call you in here about a zipper."

Xandra blinked at her. "Huh?"

"Look," Star said bluntly. "Let's get real here. I know the whole New Age thing you've got going is a big sham."

"What?" Xandra exclaimed, startled. "Why, Star, I don't know what you're—"

"Just listen, okay?" Star broke in, trying not to smile. She was sort of enjoying this so far—it felt like playing a hard-boiled type of character in an old gangster movie. "You can be straight with me, Xandra. After all, we both want the same thing."

"We—we do?" Xandra said cautiously. "Er, what do you mean?"

"Publicity." Star spat out the word like a stale piece of gum. "I've been thinking about the situation, and I'm pretty sure we can help each other out if we're honest with each other. If you come on tour with me as my personal spiritual advisor or whatever, people will eat that up. It could mean a lot of useful extra publicity for both of us. Get it?"

As Star spoke Xandra's expression had changed from confusion to cautious interest. "I'm listening," she said slowly. "But what does a celebrity at your level need with more publicity? You're already front-page news as it is."

"Hey, there's no such thing as too much publicity." Star shrugged. "Every extra photo in the paper means more tickets and CDs sold, right?"

"Sure." Xandra still looked cautious. "Um, I'm just a little surprised—I mean, you always seem so sweet, so young and innocent. . . . I had no idea you could be so, you know, cold-blooded. No offense."

Star shrugged. "None taken," she said. "I've got my image just like you've got yours. So anyway, take a moment to think about it if you need to. The offer's on the table."

Xandra was starting to look excited. "Ooh, this is good," she murmured, rubbing her hands together. "This is beyond good. I can finally ditch that walking ego, Eddie, and get some decent exposure, maybe land a few acting gigs . . ."

"Sure," Star said. Feeling a sudden twinge of guilt about what she was doing, she reminded herself that Xandra had given her little choice. "Plus, more people will buy your book, right?"

Xandra grimaced and waved one hand dismissively. "That piece of junk?" she said. "Once I'm famous for real, I'd be happy if every copy of that book disappeared forever. I'm way beyond sick of all that New Age mumbo jumbo—I can't believe there are suckers out there who actually buy into that stupid beads-and-auras crap." Suddenly seeming to remember that Star was there, she smiled obsequiously at her. "Now thanks to you, I can finally—"

"Surprise!"

Xandra spun around, gasping, as a couple of women stepped out of the nearby toilet stalls, wearing press tags around their necks and holding their cameras and tape recorders at the ready.

"Say cheese," one of them said, raising her camera to capture the look of horror on Xandra's face.

Nine

"What's going on here?" Xandra cried, sounding panicky. "Who are you? How did you get in here? This is an outrage!"

The second woman snapped several pictures as well. "Just doing our job, ma'am," she said gruffly.

"But—but I didn't give you permission to record me!" Xandra's green eyes were frantic, and she glanced around the bathroom wildly, like an animal trapped in a too-small cage. "You can't do that! Give me those tapes!"

She lunged forward, but the women were too quick for her. They jumped back out of the way. "Sorry, miss," the first one said briskly. "Public place and all that."

For a second Star thought Xandra might rush at them again, and she prepared to hurry out and call Tank before things got out of control. But that turned out not to be necessary. Xandra's expression suddenly shifted from fearful to crafty. She cleared her throat and took a step back.

"Okay, you caught me," she said more calmly. "But listen. We're all businesswomen here, right? So what will it take for me to get those tapes, hmm? Money? I can get you that. I'll even throw in an exclusive interview with Eddie Urbane if you like—I can get you that, too."

"Sorry," the second reporter mumbled. "Not interested."

"Come on!" Desperation crept back into Xandra's voice. "Everyone has a price. Just name it, okay?"

Even though Xandra was turning out to be even more of a fraud than she'd thought, Star couldn't help feeling sorry for her. "Listen, Xandra," she began.

"Quiet," Xandra snarled. "You're the one who got me into this mess, you little twit."

The comment made Star feel a lot less sorry for her. But she continued nonetheless. "I really think you'll want to hear this," she told Xandra firmly. "See, these aren't real reporters."

"What?" Xandra sounded confused. She looked from the women to Star and back again. "What are they, then, robots? Holographs?"

"I think you mean holo*grams*," the second reporter put in. "A hologram is a three-dimensional image. A holo*graph* is a type of document, one that—"

"Shut up!" Xandra cried, putting her hands to her temples. "What are you, my vocabulary teacher?"

Star grinned. "No, but she's mine," she said. "Xandra, I'd like you to meet Mrs. Magdalene Nattle, my tutor." She pointed to the other woman. "And that's Lola LaRue, my stylist."

Xandra blinked, looking more confused than ever. "Huh?"

"I asked them to put on disguises and pose as reporters. See, I figured out that you weren't really interested in being my friend or helping me find my family." She touched her necklace, which gave her strength to continue despite Xandra's deepening scowl. "All you're interested in is the publicity you can get from hanging around me. And you pretty much admitted that just now."

"On tape," Lola put in helpfully, patting the small cassette recorder slung over her shoulder on a long strap.

Xandra glared at her. "I can't believe this," she huffed, her cheeks turning bright red. "Of all the sneaky, low-down tricks . . ."

Star took a deep breath. "I'm not finished," she said firmly. "I want you to promise to leave me alone from now on. I won't be your publicity stunt. When I'm friends with someone, celebrity or not, it's always for real." Her mind flashed briefly to her friends back home, then to other friends she'd made since becoming famous—Jade, Ky, and others. "Anyway, if you don't tell anyone about all this, I won't either. Do we have a deal?"

Xandra just stared at her for a long moment, her pretty face wearing a mulish expression. But finally she nodded. "What choice do I have?" she snapped.

"Good." Star's hands and knees were shaking slightly, but she did her best not to let it show. "Then I guess we have a deal."

"Fine," Xandra snapped. "I hope you're proud of yourself, little girl."

Star took a half step backward, a bit frightened by the venom in Xandra's voice and expression. But Xandra was already turning away and stalking toward the door. A second later she was gone.

"Nice work, babydoll!" Lola exclaimed, hurrying forward to give Star a hug. "You were magnificent—so calm, so in control. Even though that Xandra woman turned out to be such a nut."

"She certainly does seem to be an unsavory piece of work," Mags agreed, peeling off the wig she was wearing and shaking out her hair. "And you're well to be rid of her, Star. As my late husband Colonel Nattle used to say, it's best not to associate with someone you wouldn't trust to hold your wallet."

Star just nodded, unable to speak for a moment. Even though she'd already figured out that Xandra was a fraud, it was still rather shocking to see her at her worst. Finally she found her voice. "I knew she didn't really want to be my friend," she said. "But I never would have guessed she was so mean underneath all that peace-and-love talk. For once I actually feel kind of sorry for Eddie, for getting stuck with her. He might be kind of conceited and a little bit of a jerk sometimes, but he's not *that* bad. . . ."

"Don't worry your cute little head about him," Lola told her. "I seriously doubt he's in that relationship for true love any more than she is."

Star sighed, knowing Lola was probably right. If Eddie followed his usual pattern, he would probably get bored with Xandra and dump her before long. That didn't make her feel much better about the whole situation, though. Why couldn't people just be honest and follow their true feelings? It would make the world a lot easier to understand.

"Come along," Mags said, breaking into Star's thoughts. "We'd better get out there before Tank starts to worry."

Lola tweaked one of Star's curls. "She's right," she said. "Besides, it's almost time to leave for the funeral, and we still need to get you dressed."

Star Power

☆ ☆ ☆ ☆ ☆

"What a lovely ceremony that was," Mags commented quietly as she stepped out into the lobby of the funeral home.

Star nodded. She looked down and smoothed the folds of her black dress, thinking about the funeral that had just ended. Even though many of those in attendance were celebrities, it had been the first event of the week that hadn't felt like just another photo op. The speakers' memories of Ernie Golden had painted a picture of a man who had been much more than a successful and wealthy producer. He had also been a friend, a brother, an uncle, a neighbor, a mentor, and much more to many, many people, only some of them famous.

He had a long, full life, Star told herself. *And not all of it had to do with show business. He made room for everything he thought was important, and that's pretty cool.*

The rest of her team seemed to be lost in their own thoughts. Mike and Mags looked dignified and solemn in their dark clothes as they led the way toward the exit. Tank hadn't said a word in any language since the end of the funeral. Even Lola seemed much more subdued than usual, with her brightly colored dreadlocks tucked under a black scarf and a gloomy expression on her face.

As they neared the door Mike glanced around at them. "All right, people," he said. "Like it or not, we've got to go out there and face the press, and then the reception. Besides, I knew Ernie pretty well, and he wouldn't want us to stay blue for long. He'd tell us to think well of the dead, then go on out there and enjoy living. *Carpe diem!*"

Star smiled up at her manager, grateful for his ability to know exactly what to say in every situation. "*Carpe diem!*" she repeated with a rush of feeling. "Come on, let's go!"

After the solemn ceremony they'd just witnessed, it seemed strange to emerge into the usual glare of paparazzi flashbulbs. But Star did her best to act normal, posing for pictures and answering a few questions about the funeral before hurrying out to the limo that would carry them to the reception back at the hotel.

Soon they were all stepping into the ballroom once again. It was already crowded with people in dark suits and dresses, though this time the paparazzi had been mostly banished to the hall outside. One of the first people Star spotted was Xandra, who was wearing a gauzy black gown with a mostly see-through skirt. She was talking animatedly with a tall, balding man Star vaguely recognized as an award-winning songwriter. Eddie was nowhere in sight.

Star braced herself as she and her team stepped closer to the pair. The songwriter nodded politely to Star and Mike, though Xandra didn't even turn in their direction as they walked by. But Star thought she caught the young woman's green eyes flickering toward her for a split second before returning to her companion.

Whew, Star thought as she followed Mike farther into the room. *Maybe that means she's going to stick to her word and stay out of my way.*

She still felt kind of strange about that. As far as she knew, she'd never had a real enemy before, at least not for long. . . . That reminded her of Jade and the early days of their complicated friendship. There was no sign of Jade anywhere in view, though Star did spot Stan Starkey and Manda standing nearby looking vaguely irritated as they stared around the crowded room.

"There's Athena," Mike said, nodding toward the center of the room. Athena was there, looking as magnificent as ever in a flowing black gown with silver trim. "Want to go say howdy?"

Not allowing herself a chance to start feeling nervous, Star nodded quickly. This could be her last chance to speak to Athena before they all left London. "Let's go," she told Mike.

Over the Top

The diva smiled graciously as Star approached her. Mike and the others hung back a few feet with Athena's bodyguards, allowing Star and Athena a moment of privacy. "Hello again, my dear," the diva said. "It was a wonderfully touching ceremony, wasn't it?"

"Definitely," Star said. "Even though I didn't know Mr. Golden well, I can tell I would have liked him a lot."

"I'm sure he would have adored you, too." Athena's smile broadened. "He always did appreciate young talent, you know."

"I've heard that. And thanks." Star took a deep breath. "Listen, Ms. Quincy. I know this probably isn't the coolest time to be doing this, but I really wanted to talk to you about something and I don't know if I'll have another chance anytime soon. I hope you don't mind."

Athena raised her carefully sculpted eyebrows in surprise. "What is it, my dear?"

"It's about your song, 'Star Bright,'" Star said quickly, before she lost her nerve. She touched her necklace. "I, um, well—that song has always been really special to me."

"How nice," Athena said with a smile. "It's one of my favorites too."

"See, my parents are huge fans of yours," Star went on.

"And they especially love that song. They even named me after it."

Athena gasped. "No!" she cried with delight. "Star—why, I'd heard that a time or two, but I had no idea it was true! How absolutely marvelous!"

"Anyway, I was sort of thinking about recording a cover of 'Star Bright' for my next album," Star said. "But I don't want to do it if I don't have, like, your blessing. What do you think?"

"I think that sounds like an outstanding idea," Athena declared.

Realizing she was holding her breath, Star let it out in a *whoosh* of relief. "That's great! Um, I was kind of nervous about asking you," Star admitted. "You know, because you did such an amazing version of the song, and you might not want someone like me messing it up. . . . But then I remembered that thing Mr. Golden always said. You know, *carpe diem*. So I figured, why not just go ahead and ask? At least then I'd know how you felt."

Athena put a hand to her heart. "Oh, child," she said with a smile. "How could I say no after hearing how much the song means to you? I'm so honored that you even felt you needed to ask. I can't wait to hear your version!"

"Thanks!" Star blurted out, relief and happiness flooding through her. "Thanks a zillion, Ms. Quincy! You're the best."

"Oh, I know." Athena threw back her head and let out a hearty laugh, ignoring the surprised looks from several bystanders. "And please—call me Athena, all right?"

Star wasn't quite sure she could do that, but she nodded. "Thanks again," she said, practically bursting with excitement. "Thank you so much."

At that moment several other guests hurried over, wanting to talk to Athena, and Star's private moment with the diva ended. But she didn't really mind. She was so overwhelmed with joy, thankfulness, and all sorts of other emotions that she wasn't sure she could have said anything coherent at that point anyway.

She hurried out into the crowd and rejoined her team. "How'd it go, sugar?" Lola asked.

"Great!" Star blurted out, grinning from ear to ear. "She loved the idea."

"Sweet!" Lola cried happily, clapping her hands. "I knew she would. That Athena Quincy always seemed like a woman of taste."

As the others added their comments and congratulations, Star couldn't seem to stop shivering with excitement. She wrapped her arms around herself, but that didn't do any good. What she needed was a few moments alone to collect her thoughts.

"Excuse me," she told her team. "I'm just going to the bathroom for a sec, okay?"

"Want me to come with?" Lola asked. She winked. "That way I'll be a witness in case a certain New Age loony follows you in and tries to start any trouble."

Star giggled. "No thanks, Lola," she said. "I think I'll be fine on my own."

She followed a nearby restroom sign and soon found herself entering a quiet hallway. A large sign on the wall just inside read MEN'S AND LADIES' RESTROOMS, SUPPLY CLOSET, BASEMENT ACCESS DOOR, COAT CHECK (CLOSED). NO OUTLET. After turning several corners and passing doors leading to most of the other places on the list, she finally spotted the ladies' room sign just ahead. As she reached out her hand to push it open, she paused, a sound catching her ear. It sounded like a low voice murmuring, and it seemed to be coming from around the next corner. She stopped and listened. The murmuring stopped, but she could hear shuffling noises, as if someone was moving around nearby.

Weird, Star thought, curious and slightly nervous. *Who*

would be back here right now? The only thing that should be up ahead is the coat check room, and according to the sign, that's not even open tonight. . . .

She stepped forward cautiously, wondering if she might find a nest of renegade rats or squirrels back there in the empty coat room. Or worse yet, a group of especially sneaky paparazzi waiting to pounce . . .

As she rounded the corner she immediately saw that it was neither. She gasped, both hands flying to her mouth in surprise. "What are you guys doing?" she cried without thinking.

Eddie Urbane and Jade flew apart in mid-kiss, both looking just as startled as Star felt.

Ten

"Hey!" Eddie blurted out, his face already turning bright red. "What's the big idea, sneaking up on people like that?"

Star just goggled at him, speechless. *Am I hallucinating, or did I actually just interrupt Eddie and Jade making out?* she thought, hardly hearing Eddie's irritated words.

Jade poked Eddie in the shoulder, tossing her dark hair out of her face. "Don't get mad at her," she said breathlessly. "I told you someone might find us back here."

"But what—," Star began. "Why . . . How—"

Eddie sighed loudly, running his fingers through his hair. "Look, sweetheart," he told Star wearily. "Don't get jealous, okay? I know you've always had the hots for me, but . . ."

Star rolled her eyes. Then she glanced at Jade. "Come on," she said. "What's going on here? Really?"

Jade shrugged, not quite meeting Star's gaze. "Whatever," she muttered. "We're just, like, hanging out, okay? No big deal."

Eddie slung his arm over Jade's shoulders. "That's right," he told Star proudly. "See, Jade here has exquisite taste in men—that's why she practically mauled me at that little lunch party thing Xandra threw yesterday. Right, babe?" He squeezed her tighter.

Star held back a smile. Obviously Eddie had no idea that Star had asked Jade to distract him the day before. *Guess they ended up distracting each other,* she thought. *Who would have guessed?*

"But that was only yesterday," she said. "You mean you guys got to know each other enough in that amount of time to . . . well, you know." She waved a hand at them.

"We sat together at the thing last night too, remember?" Jade put in, sounding slightly defensive. "That was a long show. Gave us plenty of time to get better acquainted." She shrugged and smirked. "We just had to be careful not to let Stan see it happening right under his nose."

Star shook her head, still feeling confused. Stan wasn't the only one who'd been fooled. "But why hide it from him, of all people?" she asked. "Isn't this exactly the kind of thing he wanted?"

"Yeah," Jade said shortly. "That's why."

"Oh, I see." Star shook her head. "Wait, no I don't. What are you talking about?"

Jade sighed loudly and leaned against Eddie, who still had his arm around her. "Look," she said. "I'm not doing this for the publicity, okay? That's why I don't want Stan's greasy little hands all over it. He'll just turn it into some kind of lame photo op, you know?"

Star nodded, finally understanding—at least partly. She glanced over at Eddie. "And that's okay with you?" she asked, trying not to sound accusatory. "You don't mind sneaking around in secret?"

"No way." He smiled down at Jade, suddenly looking a lot less smarmy and a lot more sincere than he usually did. "Jade's different, you know? Not like the other chicks I've dated. She's cool. I don't want to blow it by bringing the whole world into our business." He glared at Star. "And we were doing pretty well at that until you came along."

Star blinked, surprised to find that she actually believed what he was saying. Mostly, anyway. She couldn't quite forget his track record entirely—not to mention the fact that as far as most of the world knew, he was still dating Xandra.

I really hope this isn't another one of his publicity stunts, she thought with a flash of concern for the other girl. *Jade likes to act tough, but I think she'd probably be really hurt if he turns out to be using her. . . . Still, I guess I have to believe he's for real until*

I find out otherwise. I have to believe they're both actually crazy about each other.

She shook her head, amazed. A romance between Eddie Urbane and Jade . . . it was just about the last thing she ever could have imagined. But there it was, right in front of her. "Well, congratulations," she said lamely. "Um, sorry to interrupt and stuff."

Jade shrugged off Eddie's arm and stepped forward, grabbing Star by the arm. "Yo, you're not going to tell anyone, are you?" she asked, her dark eyes anxious.

"You mean the paparazzi? Or Stan? Of course not," Star assured her. "Your secret's safe with me."

"Not just them," Jade said urgently. "You've got to swear you won't tell *anyone*. Not even, like, your own people. You know?"

"But why?" Star asked, astonished by the request. "My team wouldn't tell on you any more than I would."

Eddie frowned. "Look, she's asking you for a favor," he said. "And so am I. How hard can it be to keep this to yourself?"

Star hesitated, knowing that neither of them could really understand. They weren't that close to their management teams, but Mike, Mags, Tank, and Lola were Star's family, just

131

as much as her missing parents and brother. She didn't like keeping secrets from them.

Jade took a step closer, blinking at Star. "Please, Star?" she said. "I know it's totally bent and all. But we just want to give this thing a chance, figure it out before anyone else knows about it, okay?"

"Yeah, I guess I get it," Star said slowly. She really was starting to understand. It would have been even harder to figure out how she felt about Aaron back home if they'd first met when she was already famous. Besides, she couldn't help feeling at least partially responsible for Jade and Eddie being together in the first place. After all, if she'd never asked Jade to distract Eddie the day before, the two of them might never have discovered that they liked each other.

"So, is that a promise?" Eddie demanded. "You've got to swear to keep quiet. If Starkey finds out . . ."

Star ignored him, suddenly remembering something else she'd wanted to say to Jade. "Hey, listen," she told her. "About last night—I'm really sorry I gave you away to Stan. You know, when you told him you were with me or whatever. I felt terrible when I realized what was up."

"No big." Jade glanced at Eddie. "Eddie and I were together, in case you didn't figure that out."

Star blinked, realizing that she hadn't. But now it all made sense. "Well, anyway, I'm really sorry," she said. "Stan seemed so mad . . ."

Jade shrugged and smiled tightly, staring at the wall somewhere beyond Star's left shoulder. "Like I said, no big," she said. "I didn't give you a heads-up or anything—not your fault."

Star bit her lip, not quite daring to say anything else. Jade's clipped words and the tight, uncomfortable look on her face made it clear that she didn't want to talk about the incident with her manager.

"Okay," Star said softly, suddenly feeling very closed off from the other girl. "I just wanted to say I was sorry, that's all."

Jade nodded. Then her eyes flicked over to meet Star's for a moment, and she smiled slightly. "It's all good," she said. "And don't worry—next time I use you as an alibi, I'll be sure to let you know, okay?"

Star smiled back at her. "Deal," she said. Jade might be a difficult sort of friend—complicated, a bit prickly, downright hard to understand at times. But Star was still pretty sure she was worth it.

"Look, are you going to promise to keep quiet, or not?" Eddie burst out, sounding impatient.

Star realized she'd almost forgotten he was there. She stared at him, once again wondering if he could possibly be sincere about his interest in Jade. He glared back at her suspiciously.

"Yo," he said. "Look, Calloway. I know you probably have it in for me, after . . ." He glanced quickly at Jade, then returned his gaze to Star and shrugged. "Well, you know. Stuff. But you don't have to take it out on Jade by ratting us out, you know?"

Star hid a smile. Clearly Eddie hadn't yet told Jade certain things about his short but interesting history with Star—like the time he'd tried to sabotage her tour, or the time he'd let the world think he and Star were dating, or the time he'd dognapped Dudley . . .

Her smile faded as she recalled just how sneaky and self-centered Eddie could be. *I hope Jade knows what she's in for,* she thought. *I really hope she doesn't let Eddie take advantage of her or hurt her.*

"Well?" Eddie demanded, still glaring at Star. "You going to answer me, or what?"

Jade poked him in the shoulder, hard enough that he winced and stepped away from her. "Hey," she said. "Get off her case, okay? Star's cool; she'll do the right thing. You don't have to get all up in her grille about it like some kind of spaz."

Eddie frowned. "Look," he whined. "I just wanted to make sure . . ."

"Well, get over it and drop it, okay?" Jade insisted. "It's getting way old."

This time Eddie just shrugged in response, looking sheepish. Once again Star was forced to hold back a grin. *Okay, so maybe I don't need to worry about Jade being able to handle Eddie,* she thought. *It seems like she knows exactly how to handle him. You never know, maybe she'll be good for him. Maybe they'll be good for each other.*

She still wasn't sure she understood or approved of Jade's choice of boyfriends. But that didn't mean she wouldn't do anything she could to help her—even if that meant keeping Jade's secret from Mike and the others.

"Neither of you have to worry," she said, ignoring the slightly uneasy feeling in the pit of her stomach. "I won't tell a soul until you give me the okay. Cross my heart."

When Star returned to the reception a few minutes later, she had overcome her misgivings and was feeling bubbly and warm over her secret romantic news. It was exciting that Jade had found someone to swoon over, even if it was only Eddie.

I wish I could tell someone, Star thought, shivering slightly with giddiness. *But since I can't, maybe it's time to get back to work on the other potential couple in the room. . . .*

She glanced around for her bodyguard. Despite her good intentions, Tank's promising friendship with the attractive young studio musician kept slipping her mind. But now that she'd remembered again, she didn't intend to rest until she figured out a way to bring the two of them together and see what happened.

I'm sure Anita is here somewhere, she thought, glancing around the crowded room. *Now all I have to do is make sure Tank spends some serious time with her, even if I have to drag all two-hundred-plus pounds of him over to her myself.*

Spotting Lola walking past carrying a glass of wine, she hurried to catch her. "Hey, have you seen Tank anywhere?" she asked.

Lola shrugged. "Sorry, babydoll," she said. "I haven't seen him since we came in. Why? Need something?"

"No, it's okay. I just wanted to tell him something. Thanks anyway." Star moved on, keeping her eyes peeled for either Tank or Anita. She asked a few other people if they'd seen him, but nobody seemed to have any idea where he might be.

As she neared the far end of the room, where a DJ was playing some of Ernie Golden's hits, Star was feeling frustrated.

She knew there was no way Tank had left the reception—not while she was still there. So why couldn't she seem to find him?

At that moment the crowd parted in front of her. She gasped. "Tank!" she blurted out, recognizing her bodyguard's stocky form just ahead.

She stared in amazement. There wasn't really a dance floor per se—after all, it was supposed to be a funeral reception, not a party. But Tank was swaying back and forth in a small area of the floor in front of the DJ's booth. His muscular arms were wrapped around the petite form of a dark-haired woman. As Star watched, he leaned down and whispered something into his partner's ear. She threw back her head and giggled, fluttering her eyelashes up at Tank while he smiled down at her. He reached up and gently pushed a strand of the woman's curly dark hair out of her face.

"Anita," Star whispered in astonishment.

She heard a soft chuckle from directly behind her. Turning, she saw Lola standing there. "Looks like you discovered Tank's secret, hmm?" Lola murmured. "Figured you would soon enough."

"But—but—what—," Star stammered, feeling perplexed at this turn of events.

Lola smiled at her. "Don't look so surprised, babydoll," she said. "Didn't Tank tell you? He and Anita there used to go out, years and years ago."

"Really?" Star blinked. "He didn't tell me."

"Oops." Lola didn't look particularly upset at having revealed Tank's secret. "Well, anyway, they were quite the couple for a while, according to those who knew him when." She winked. "Not that I'm gossiping, you understand—at least not if Mike asks."

Star smiled. "Of course not," she said. "But come on, Lola—spill. When did they hook up again?" She gestured toward Tank and Anita, who were still dancing, completely oblivious to anything but each other.

"They ran into each other at the welcome party, remember?" Lola said. "Ever since then, they've been hanging out a bit whenever they had the chance."

Star shook her head. "But when was that?" she asked. "I mean, Tank spends, like, every waking minute with me—driving me around, being my bodyguard, helping me work out . . ."

"Every waking minute of *yours*, maybe," Lola said with a wink. "I happen to know the two of them went out for a nightcap last night after you were all tucked in for the night. And they've been talking on the phone every chance they get."

"Oh." Star thought about that, realizing Tank really did have quite a bit of down time—for instance, when he waited for her while she did an interview, or sat in the car while she and Mike were having lunch with record executives or meeting with other business types. Normally he spent that kind of free time reading or listening to talk radio in whatever language he happened to find on the local dial.

But I guess for the past few days he's spent it racking up his cell phone bill talking to Anita instead, she thought, suddenly feeling sheepish. How could she not notice something like that happening right under her nose? It made her wonder how many other important things she didn't know about the adults in her life.

Lola seemed to guess some of her thoughts. "Don't be too hard on yourself, sugar," she said comfortingly. "He wasn't really trying to keep it a secret from you. He's just sort of shy about this sort of thing, you know?"

"I guess," Star said, feeling a little better.

Lola winked. "Of course, it was pretty hard to miss that moony, goofy look he's had plastered all over his face for the past two days . . . ," she added teasingly.

Star giggled. "Hey, give me a break," she teased in return. "I'm short, remember? You're lucky I know Tank even *has* a face."

"Good point," Lola said with a smile. "Besides, just because we all spend so much time together, it doesn't mean we each can't have a few secrets, right?"

Star returned her smile, thinking of her own new secret about Jade and Eddie. "Right," she agreed, automatically scanning the room to see if the two of them had reappeared yet. Then her gaze returned to Tank, and she shivered with happiness for her bodyguard.

Life sure can be interesting, she thought, *secrets and all!*

Now you can give yourself

star power

Star Power Karaoke Machine Contest

Official Rules

1. NO PURCHASE NECESSARY.

2. To enter the **STAR POWER KARAOKE MACHINE CONTEST** write your name, telephone number, and address on one side of a 3" x 5" card and mail it to: **STAR POWER KARAOKE MACHINE CONTEST**, Simon & Schuster Children's Publishing Division, Marketing Department, 1230 Avenue of the Americas, New York, New York 10020. Limit one (1) entry per person. Not responsible for: postage due; late, lost, stolen, damaged, incomplete, undelivered, mutilated, illegible, or misdirected entries; or for typographical errors in the rules. Sweepstakes starts February 22, 2005. Entries must be postmarked by May 21, 2005, and received by May 27, 2005.

3. All entries become the property of Sponsor and will not be acknowledged or returned.

4. A total of three (3) winners will be selected at random from all eligible entries received in a drawing to be held on or about June 24, 2005. Winner will be notified by U.S. mail. Odds of winning depend on the number of eligible entries received. If prize or notification is returned as undeliverable, prize will be forfeited and awarded to an alternate.

5. Prizes: A total of three (3) prizes will be awarded, each consisting of one (1) karaoke machine, three karaoke CDs for use with the machine, and a copy of one book from the Star Power series by Catherine Hapka. (Total approximate retail value $150.00 each).

6. Sweepstakes is open to legal residents of the U.S. and Canada (excluding Quebec) ages 8 to 16 as of March 1, 2005. Employees (and immediate family members or those with whom they are domiciled) of Sponsor, its parent, subsidiaries, divisions, and related companies, and their respective agencies and agents are ineligible.

7. No transfers, assignments, substitutions, or cash equivalents of prize allowed, except by Sponsor in the event of prize unavailability, in which case a prize of comparable value will be awarded. Void in Puerto Rico, Quebec, and wherever prohibited or restricted by law.

8. By participating, entrants agree to these rules and the decisions of the judges, which are final in all respects. All taxes, if any, are the sole responsibility of the winners. Winners, or the parent/legal guardian of any winner if any winner is a minor, may be required to execute and return an affidavit of eligibility and publicity/liability release within 15 days of notification attempt or an alternative winner may be selected.

9. By accepting a prize, winner grants to Sponsor the right to use his/her name and likeness for any advertising, promotional, trade, or any other purpose without further compensation or permission, except where prohibited by law.

10. If the winner is a Canadian resident, then he/she will be required to answer a time-limited skill-testing question.

11. By entering, entrants release Sponsor and its subsidiaries, affiliates, divisions, and advertising, production, and promotion agencies from any and all liability for any loss, harm, damages, costs, or expenses, including without limitation property damages, personal injury, and/or death, arising out of participation in this sweepstakes; the acceptance, possession, use, or misuse of any prize; claims based on publicity rights, defamation, or invasion of privacy; or merchandise delivery.

12. For the names of the prize winners (available after July 22, 2005) send a separate, stamped, self-addressed envelope to Winners' List, c/o **STAR POWER KARAOKE MACHINE CONTEST**, Simon & Schuster Children's Marketing Department, 1230 Avenue of the Americas, New York, New York 10020. All list requests must be received by August 31, 2005.

13. Sponsor: Simon & Schuster Children's Publishing, 1230 Avenue of the Americas, New York, NY 10020.

Aladdin Paperbacks
Simon & Schuster Children's Publishing Division
www.SimonSaysKids.com

Printed in the United States
By Bookmasters